Praise for Hope Tarr

"This entertaining
rainy afternoon w[...]
place dreaming a[...]
alpha male. I kn[...]
—Barbara V[...]
Bo[...]

"Hope Tarr is a must read in any genre,
but this one is definitely a must read and it
deserves a place on the reader's keeper shelf."
—*Romance Junkies* on *Bound to Please*

"Fury and passion go head to head in
Every Breath You Take.... The emotional swings
are dizzying, and will keep you captivated right
up until the end."
—*Coffee Time Romance*

"Tarr paints a realistic, yet beautiful picture
of a couple's struggle between chemistry,
secrets and lies."
—*Romance Novel TV* on *Every Breath You Take*

"Heartwarming characters, wonderful passion
and an innovative story make this the perfect
Christmas tale."
—*RT Book Reviews* on *It's a Wonderfully Sexy Life*

"A delightful, intriguing mix of past and present,
love and betrayal, *The Haunting* by Hope Tarr is
sure to find its way into your heart. Add this one
to your to-buy list."
—*Cataromance*

Dear Reader,

After my Scottish medieval romance, *Bound to Please*, was published, I was thrilled and humbled by the outpouring of reader e-mails asking for a sequel, one that told of the romance between bad boy Callum Fraser and Alys, the quiet maid who steals his heart. So how could I resist?

Callum, laird of Clan Fraser, and Alys, a lovely Lowlands handmaid with a dark past, first meet in the final few chapters of *Bound to Please*. Their attraction is intense and immediate, a clear case of love at first sight. At the end of the book, the pair appears destined to live happily ever after. Then again, the course of true love rarely runs smoothly, not even at Christmas.

I hope you enjoy *Twelve Nights*. And please look for my upcoming Harlequin Victorian Christmas anthology with bestselling authors Betina Krahn and Jacquie D'Alessandro, available in December 2010.

Wishing you winter holidays filled with love, laughter and sexy second chances,

Hope Tarr
www.hopetarr.com

Hope Tarr

TWELVE NIGHTS

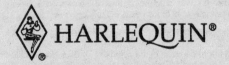

TORONTO • NEW YORK • LONDON
AMSTERDAM • PARIS • SYDNEY • HAMBURG
STOCKHOLM • ATHENS • TOKYO • MILAN • MADRID
PRAGUE • WARSAW • BUDAPEST • AUCKLAND

Recycling programs
for this product may
not exist in your area.

ISBN-13: 978-0-373-79516-1

TWELVE NIGHTS

This edition published by arrangement with Harlequin Books S.A.

® and TM are trademarks of the publisher. Trademarks indicated with ® are registered in the United States Patent and Trademark Office, the Canadian Trade Marks Office and in other countries.

www.eHarlequin.com

Printed in U.S.A.

ABOUT THE AUTHOR

Hope Tarr is an award-winning author of a dozen contemporary and historical romance novels. *Twelve Nights* is Hope's sixth book for Harlequin's sexy Blaze line and the sequel to *Bound to Please*, the first Blaze Historical. Hope lives in Manhattan where she finds the people-watching sublime and daily life more nuanced if not always stranger than fiction. She is a cofounder of Lady Jane's Salon, www.ladyjanesalon.com, Manhattan's first and so far only monthly reading series devoted to romance fiction. To enter her monthly contest or to read about her latest "single girl in the big city" adventures on her blog, visit Hope online at www.hopetarr.com.

Books by Hope Tarr

HARLEQUIN BLAZE

For POC with remembered kisses.

Prologue

Castle Fraser, Beauly
The Scottish Highlands, May 1460

CALLUM, LAIRD OF CLAN FRASER, walked toward the walled rose garden. In his mother's day it had been a lovely place, but years of neglect had rendered it a ruin. Picking his way through the weeds, he sat down on the stone bench. A single rosebush survived to grow wild in one corner. The partially opened buds put him in mind of a certain maid's petal-pink mouth. Callum had never been a slave to sentiment, but he found himself reaching out to stroke one fragile blossom.

As if his fantasy had conjured her from the air, the lady known as Alys approached. Pulling his hand back from the rose, he wondered if she'd seen him enter and followed him inside. The madness of that possibility made his pulse race.

She greeted him with a curtsy and a slight smile. "My lord."

She straightened to stand before him, the purity of her face and form stealing his breath. Dressed in a simple blue gown, a light muslin veil draping her golden tresses, she looked as though she'd stepped out of one of the stained glass windows in his chapel.

"I do not mean to disturb you—"

He rose to stand on shaking legs. "You do not." He took a step toward her.

"I am in search of my lady. I have not seen her since yesterday. Can you tell me which chamber she occupies?" Alys nibbled her bottom lip and cast her gaze away.

Her modesty disarmed him as other women's wiles never had. He wondered if she was always this shy or if perhaps, after the other day, his presence discomfited her. The latter thought snared his hopes, daring him to dream.

"I expect she is with my brother. In his bedchamber," he added out of deference to the devil driving him to see if he could make her blush.

She did not disappoint him. Pale roses nearly the same shade as her mouth climbed the trellis of her delicately boned cheeks.

"Shall I take you to her?"

She snapped up her head. Her eyes registered what looked to be alarm. "Nay, she and Lord Ewan have their own affairs to settle."

He chided himself for teasing her. Stepping back from the situation, it amazed him that he, who had boasted that his body did not possess so much as a single sentimental bone, could feel so completely tender toward this one wee woman. His heart swelled every time he looked upon her. Other parts of his anatomy swelled too but that sensation wasn't nearly as novel. None of his past dealings with women had left him feeling this way before. He yearned to lay her down upon the bench, pull down her gown and suckle her small perfect breasts, and then push her legs apart and tongue and taste and tease her woman's flesh before he finally entered her, in a climactic conquering possession. At the same time, he longed to take her in his arms and settle her on his lap and simply hold her, to tuck her head beneath his chin and shelter her against his chest like the rare treasure she was.

"Nay worries, lady. Unlike me, my brother is the kindest and gentlest of men." He felt a sudden, self-defeating need to warn her away from him.

She sent him a puzzled look. "You do not think of yourself as kind?"

He hesitated and then admitted, "Not always. Not usually." True hunters always gave their quarry a sporting chance.

She firmed her chin. "You do yourself a disservice, sir. I think you're one of the kindest men I've ever met. And one of the noblest."

Callum couldn't recall the last time someone had defended him. Never, he supposed, but then he wasn't the sort who deserved defending. "You dinna ken me well."

She stepped closer, bridging the little distance remaining between them. "It's not every man who would put his own affairs aside so selflessly to search for a brother gone missing. Nor would any man be so quick to forgive the woman who had abducted and held Lord Ewan and yet you treat milady and…and me as though we are your honored guests. A brute would have made us his prisoners."

Brianna, Laird of the MacLeods, had held his twin, Ewan, captive these past weeks, not in her dungeon but in her bed. Ostensibly the abduction was in retribution for her late husband's murder, a deed her treacherous and now dead advisor, Duncan, had laid at Callum's door. Woman or not, had she harmed so much as a hair on Ewan's head, Callum wouldn't have hesitated to shoot an arrow straight to her heart. But Callum knew his twin almost as well as he knew himself. Ewan had loved Brianna since they'd first met as children. When news of her marriage to a kinsman had reached them, his normally mellow-minded sibling had brooded for months. Once Ewan had accustomed himself to the notion, being Brianna's love slave must have seemed a dark fantasy come true. Callum ventured to guess the reunited couple was even now enjoying similar sport in Ewan's turret chamber, this time with his future sister-in-law most happily bound to Ewan's bed.

Not so very long ago, Callum would have traded places with his brother gladly. The MacLeod was a handsome woman, tall, flame-haired and generously curved. But since the other evening when he'd first set eyes upon her handmaid, Alys, a pocket-sized Venus garbed as a groomsman and fleeing with her mistress, his passions ran to pale golden hair, delicate features and a fairy's form.

He took a step toward her, shaking his head. "I ken you are one of those rare women who see only the good in people. And you are so very young." She looked all of sixteen though her bearing told him she must be older.

She focused her gaze on the ground. Long lashes

tipped in gold cast shadows over the tops of her fine-boned cheeks. "Young and ignorant though I am, I have seen aplenty of that which is bad."

She looked up, eyes brimming. A tear slid down her cheek. Watching the progress of that single, crystalline droplet all but tore at him. He lifted his hand to her cheek.

"How now, lady, why the tears?" Her flushed flesh felt satin smooth against his palm.

She shook her head. "You treat me as a lady because you are so good and kind, but I am not as I seem. I have a son. His name is Alasdair. Even though his late father and I were duly wed, no good household would take us in. I plied the harlot's trade to keep us."

The misery in her eyes and the trembling of her lower lip cut through the last cordon of his self-control. He stroked his knuckles down her jaw to her chin. Tilting her heart-shaped face up to his, he looked into her eyes. "It seems to me you are a mother who so loves her child that she would sacrifice her own good for his."

Her mouth curved into a small smile. She shook her head, the movement splashing a tear onto his wrist. "Now which of us is determined to see only the good? And yet you say you are not kind, my lord."

He leaned in, his mouth hovering but a hairsbreadth from hers. "I have not always been kind. In the past I have been prideful and boastful and selfish to a fault. I have bullied and blustered and seized what I wanted without thought or care for the consequences. But with you at my side, sweet Alys, I believe I could learn to be a better man."

"My lord?" Startled blue eyes flew to his.

Rather than reply in words, Callum bent his head and laid siege to her rosebud mouth with a gentle, yet demanding kiss.

1

Seven months later
December 24, Christmas Eve

I BELIEVE I could learn to be a better man.

Pacing the corridor outside his lady's solar on their wedding eve, his bride gift bundled beneath one arm, Callum Fraser realized that seven months of self-imposed celibacy had put his newfound goodness to a mighty test.

It seemed an eternity since that May Day when he'd dropped down on bended knee and proposed. "Marry me, sweet Alys, for I love thee true."

Tears shone in her beautiful blue eyes. She nodded fiercely. "I love you, too, my lord, with all my heart. And I will consent to be your wife on two conditions."

Conditions! Accustomed to seizing what he wanted, he hadn't expected any caveats nor did he care for the prospect of bargaining with his bride.

Still, desperate as he was to have her, he hadn't hesitated. "Anything, my dearling, anything you wish. You've only to name it."

Her heart-shaped face had registered both steely resolve and shy sweetness. "I canna bring a maidenhead to our bridal bed, but I would come to you as a true bride, untouched by you."

Awash in finer feelings, he'd nodded, thinking to set the wedding date for soon, *very* soon. "If that is what you wish, then you have my word it shall be so."

"I thank you." She sent him a small, relieved smile. "Secondly, I would have us marry at Christmastide, so that I may be your Christmas gift and you mine."

Taken aback, he'd risen quickly, nearly falling over on his side. "But Alys, my sweet, Christmastide is a full seven months away."

Her firm little nod sent his soul sinking. "Aye, milord, and in those seven months we both shall know whether or not you've given your pledge in haste." Her face shadowed. "I married in haste once before, taking my vows at an inn instead of a church and finding myself a widow before I had the chance to truly be a wife. I canna regret a union that brought me my son, still, the matter came to a sorry end." The plaintive look she sent him slashed at his heart.

He'd had no choice but to give way. "Then let the nuptials take place upon the First Day of Christmas, my lady, for I mean for us to disport ourselves most merrily, most wickedly, on each of the twelve feast days—and nights."

There had followed the longest seven months of his life.

Seven months of chaste kisses. Seven months of lonely nights and spotty sleep. Seven months of awaking from fevered dreams in which Alys lay beside him, beneath him, astride him. Seven months of cursing himself for making a promise that neither of them had really wanted him to keep. Now he was weary of waiting, weary of wanting, and altogether weary of doing without. Mere minutes stood between him and midnight, and their wedding day. Why bother with waiting at all?

Creaking drew his gaze to the slowly opening door. He fell back into the darkened archway, dodging the sudden splash of light. Milread, his sister-in-law Brianna's wise woman, poked her head out, her white hair streaming beyond her humped back.

"Dinna fret, wean, like as not the little lordling sleeps still, but I'll go to him to be sure." She turned back inside the chamber, proffering a profile of warty nose and pointed chin. "Bide here and bolt the door 'til I return. I dinna trust that randy bridegroom of yours any farther than I can throw him."

Callum bristled. Since her arrival that morning, Milread had kept Alys confined within her chamber, supposedly as a safeguard against ill luck. Near sightless and almost toothless, still the old dragon made for a formidable foe.

"Milread, truly, is that entirely necessary?" Frustration strained Alys's dulcet voice. "My lord has already seen me. We broke our fast together in his great hall this very morn."

"My lady Brianna sent me in her stead to see you kept safe, and safe you will be kept. Marriage is a tricky enough matter without courting bad luck to begin it."

Callum caught his sweetheart's sigh just before the door fell closed. The bolt struck home. Cursing silently, he held his breath and waited. The crone passed him by,

her small, crooked shadow cutting a goblinlike sil-
houette on the stone wall, her shambling gait carrying
her with infuriating slowness toward the opposite
corridor where Alys's son's nursery lay. The second she
was out of sight, he stepped out into the open.

A pox on old wives' warnings! A man fashioned his
own fortunes. Callum marched up to the door, feeling his
resolve firm along with other oh so sensitive parts. He was
laird, was he not? Really, who was there to stay him?

He set his fist upon the planked wood and laid siege.

SITTING BEFORE HER DRESSING MIRROR stroking the
ivory-backed brush through her freshly washed hair,
Alys marveled at what a difference seven months had
made. Less than a year ago she'd barged into Brianna's
great hall, a penniless prostitute come to plead for the
return of her baby from the burgher's widow who'd
stolen him. Now she was about to marry the man of her
dreams, a lord who not only loved and honored her but
who also wished to be a father to her son. The sight of
Alasdair being carried about the castle grounds on her
beloved's broad shoulders never failed to bring grateful
tears to her eyes. Her boy wouldn't be a bairn forever.
At only thirteen months, already he'd begun showing
signs of willfulness that needed the guidance of a strong
yet loving man. Callum might not be her son's natural
sire, yet Alys felt sure a better father could not be found.

That their wedding celebration would last the full
twelve days of Christmas seemed only fitting. With
Callum as her husband, Christmas promised to take place
not only for the traditional twelve days but all three

hundred and sixty-five. He'd already pledged to present her with a different sensual "gift" on each of their first twelve nights together, gifts they would savor and enjoy throughout the years. Considering all the wicked things she'd dreamt of doing with him, her pulse skipped every time she imagined what the next twelve nights might bring. And yet ever since breaking her fast that morning, foreboding had seized hold of her, jangling her nerves and seeping into her bones like a dank, dark mist. No doubt it was nothing more than a bride's natural nervousness, but she couldn't help wishing they'd set the wedding for Christmastide Eve instead.

Pummeling outside her door startled her, causing the comb to slip from her fingers. She rose from the cushioned bench on jellied legs. Callum! It must be. The only other who would come to her chamber at this hour was Milread, and it was too soon for the wise woman to have returned.

Callum's muffled shout confirmed it. "Alys, 'tis me."

She hurried over to the bolted door, the desire to see him warring with the desire to keep their love safe. For a betrothed couple to see one another on the eve of their nuptials was to risk the ultimate bad fortune. She'd disregarded tradition in her first marriage and there'd been the very devil to pay. This time she meant to do everything proper and right.

Through the barrier, she called back, "My lord, you must leave at once, for 'tis terrible ill luck for you to see me the night before our wedding."

Ever stubborn, he shouted at what must be the tops of his lungs, "Nay worries, lady, for 'tis after midnight and thus morn already. I would but claim a Christmas kiss from your sweet lips."

Despite her fears, she chuckled. "Quiet you, my lord. You'll wake the household entire."

"And if I do, 'tis mine to wake as I will."

She pressed the side of her cheek against the planked wood, wishing it were Callum. The glimpse she'd got when they'd broken their fast that morning seemed so very long ago.

"I will grant you all the kisses you desire tomorrow eve, after our vows are said and the Yule candle lit." At that moment a chill swept across her back and the shiver kept her from saying more.

He honeyed his voice. "I have a gift for you, and it willna wait."

"Another gift!" She pulled back from the door. "You are too good to me."

Her cedar-lined cupboard and bride's chest were both bursting with his bounty. It wasn't yet the first day of Christmas and already several sumptuous gifts had found their way into her room: a cowl encrusted with semiprecious stones, a pair of slippers stitched with scarlet silk and soled of softest leather, a mahogany inlaid sewing chest filled with an array of various sized bodkins, a pair of silver scissors and spools of fancy spun thread.

"That would be impossible. You are the sweetest, kindest and aye, fairest lady in all of Christendom, and I the most fortunate of men. Only set aside these fears of old wives' warnings and let me in, sweeting. I willna claim more than kisses. Just kisses, only kisses, I swear to you."

Alys bit her bottom lip. Oh, she was tempted—

sorely. The seven months of waiting had been power-fully hard on her, too. She could scarcely credit it. Her one taste of passion had been with her English husband, Alexander, and they'd been together mere months when he'd left her in the port city of Portree on the Isle of Skye and returned to the service of the English lord to whom he owed fealty as a foot soldier. Soon after he'd con-tracted the smallpox and died, leaving her alone in a strange city with their newborn son. Scarcely risen a week from childbed, she'd spent one of her last precious coins on the bolt of saffron cloth that, once fashioned into a kirtle, would proclaim her as a whore. During those dark days of walking the docks, she'd kept her body numb, her mind blank, and her heart sealed off to anyone save her son. She'd thought herself forever ruined as a woman, too jaded for passion and too bitter for love. But these past seven months of holding Callum to his promise had proven her wrong. For the first time in her life, she knew what it meant to long for someone with all her body, all her mind and aye, all her heart. The sound of his voice through the door sufficed to send warmth flooding her heart and her nether parts in equal measure. Her breasts tingled, her womanhood wept, her empty arms and all the rest of her ached to be filled.

She gave up, surrendered. "One kiss and then you must take your leave."

She lifted the bolt and stepped back. With Callum there was no such thing as stopping at a single kiss, and well they both knew it.

The door flew open. Callum launched himself across the threshold. "Alys, dearling!" He dropped his bundle atop the trestle table, kicked the door closed behind him, and swept her into his arms. Lifting her from her feet, he swung her around. "It feels a lifetime since last I saw you." He set her down and held her away from him, regarding her with burning blue eyes fringed with wicked black lashes. "How have you been keeping yourself since this morn? They've treated you well, have they? I ordered that you be tended as befits not only a laird's lady but a queen."

As always, his tenderness melted her. So long as they stopped with kisses, she would give him as many as he wanted.

She stroked one side of his face, so handsome and so very dear to her, and admitted, "I am not accustomed to being so coddled."

The warm milk-water bath with rose petals, the massage with scented oils rubbed into her fire-warmed flesh, and finally the supper served upon a silver tray in her room had been lovely but overwhelming. And thanks to the services of the nimble little maid he'd insisted on giving her, her best blue gown now hung on a peg to warm before the fire, the rich brocade thoroughly brushed. Callum had pressed her to accept a bolt of cloth of gold and make a new gown from it, but in this she'd refused him. Cloth of gold was reserved for the nobility, but it wasn't humility that held her back. The shimmering fabric reminded her of the bold yellow gown she'd worn when she'd plied the harlot's trade. When she'd entered Brianna's household as a servant, she'd seized her first opportunity to stitch herself a simple blue gown from cloth she'd scavenged from the scrap heap and tossed the hated yellow one into the fire.

Not yellow, not ever again.

His big, warm hands spanned her waist. Of all the men who'd put their hands upon her, her husband included, no one had ever made her feel so wholly safe, so beautifully loved.

He ran his gaze along the length of her, lingering on the swell of her breasts above her shift's smocked bodice, his blue eyes undressing her as surely as his hands would this time tomorrow. "Such a slip of a thing you are, my lady, a wee wisp of a woman, and yet you fill my heart so full that betimes I fear to burst with the love I feel for you."

He still hadn't kissed her. Knowing his wicked ways, she more than suspected he held off deliberately, making her want it, making her want him.

And Alys did want him, oh how she wanted. Her nipples ached, her womanhood throbbed and her mind, dear Lord, her mind… Like flood waters rushing past the failed barrier of a broken dam, her mind fair near to burst with all manner of delicious, devil-made images… Registering the surprise on his handsome face when instead of pulling away she pushed him back against the wall… Drawing up his kilt and tearing off her smock… Smelling his desire, savoring his brine… Straddling him and moving his callused hands to cup her bottom… Spearing him inside her, that first delicious sharp thrust. Were it not for her fear of tempting fickle Fate, she'd gladly forgo any further waiting, forgo any further wanting, and play out every sinfully lovely fantasy.

"Oh, Callum." She let out a choked sob and lifted her head from his chest, trusting herself even less than she did him. "Claim your kiss, my lord, for after it you must make good on your promise and go away."

"Must I?" He lifted her one hand from his chest, turned it over, and kissed the sensitive spot on her palm.

Like one of the archery arrows he so unerringly aimed, the sensation struck straight to her core, raising a blaze of heat, a void of blinding wanting. Imagining him filling her, easing her, stroking her slowly back and forth, she shivered. "Aye, you must. Milread will return at any time."

Callum snorted and reached for her other hand. "I can more than manage one old woman. 'Tis the young and beautiful woman before me that tests my true limits." Teasing her thumb with the tip of his tongue, he looked up at her through the veil of his black lashes.

She felt her knees weaken, taking her good intentions along with them. And yet she must be strong. There was so very much at stake, so very much to lose. She'd learned that the hard way. By the time she and her first husband, Alex, had reached Skye, their babe, Alasdair, was already big in her belly. As Alex had pointed out, they couldn't possibly hope to marry in a sanctuary, not with her in such a state of obvious disgrace. Instead they'd wed in the public room of an inn in Portree, the ceremony performed by a priest from St. Andrew's whom Alex had bribed. She'd never been able to entirely shake off the shame of that sad little ceremony—or recover from the far greater shame that was soon to follow.

"My lord, you must go." She shoved at his chest.

He didn't budge. "And you, my wee bride, must call me Callum." He punctuated the command with a wink.

"Very well, Callum, I pray you rise and go—now!"

He let out a laugh and cut his gaze downward to the bulge tenting his kilt. "I assure you, lady, I *am* rising. But first your gift."

He wasn't lying. Through the scratchy wool of his kilt, she could feel his hardness rubbing the bottom half of her belly. Imagining how wondrous fine that thick rod would feel, she closed her eyes and willed herself to be strong. This time, she must take no chances. For both their sakes.

The sound of rustling had her opening her eyes. Callum handed her the bundle he'd brought. She'd been so ensnared by her lustful thoughts, she'd as good as forgotten it.

"Thank you."

She took the package, testing its weight. It was light. She almost wondered if the wrapping cloth might not outstrip its contents. Thinking it must be a toy for Alasdair, she unwound the strip of linen. The cloth fell away. She held the gift up to better catch the light. The flickering flames revealed the ugliest doll she'd ever beheld. Small and crudely formed, it was a female figure hewn of hoary wood.

Aware of Callum's expectant gaze upon her, she hesitated, unsure of what to say. "It is verra…unusual." She surveyed the creature's enormous crooked nose and slit-like eyes. "Alasdair is surely asleep, but I will give it to him first thing on the morrow."

"Alasdair?" He stared at her strangely. "But 'tis for you, my love."

Without warning, he tossed back his head and roared. He laughed so long and so hard that even loving him as she did she was tempted to crack the ugly thing over his head.

Swiping a hand across watery eyes, he straightened his face. "Wheesht, 'tis the Christmas Old Wife. I fashioned her for you this verra eve with wood from a withered stump. Do you nay have the custom in the Lowlands?"

She shook her head. "Nay, we dinna, leastways not when I lived there."

He took the figure from her. Holding it at arm's length, he surveyed his handiwork with a smile. "Looks a whit like Milread, aye?"

She opened her mouth to reprimand him but before she could, he drew back and hurled the figurine across the room. It landed neatly in the fire, the flames eating through it along with the peat.

It was too late and yet reflexively she grabbed for his arm. "What'd you go and do that for!"

Wicked blue eyes met hers. "'Tis the custom, lass. The Christmas Old Wife stands for the evils of winter and death. The burning is said to ward off misfortune for the coming year. And my sweet Alys, I mean for these next twelve months to be wicked wondrous indeed, starting with these coming twelve nights. Better yet, why do we nay start our celebrating…now?" His gaze brushed over her bare shoulders and then dropped.

Feeling her morals slipping along with her smock, she tugged the bodice back up. "I'm nay sure I should marry a man who treats his wives so poorly. How do I know you'll not cast me aside, too, once I'm withered and old?"

He braced a hand on either side of the wall behind her head, trapping her between his arms. "You could never be withered and even were you to become so, I would always treat you as the rare and precious treasure you are."

There was no means of escape in sight and were she honest with herself, she must admit she had never wanted less to escape in all her life. She looked up into his handsome face beaming with masculine confidence, and felt her heart twist with love and her body blossom with lust. Milread had the right of it. The devil surely did make them bonny. And Callum didn't only look good. He *smelled* good, too, better than any man to whom she'd ever been this close. The strong clean scent of evergreen mingled with the scents of leather and musk to create a scent that was savory, not sweet. Nay, most definitely not sweet.

She shook her head, more than halfway to drunk on him. "Oh, Callum, must I really be good for the both of us?"

His smile broadened to a full-blown grin of generous lips and even teeth. "Alys, my dearling, I dinna wish for you to be good at all. Now kiss me, sweetheart, for sure you ken what mistletoe is for?"

Caught off guard, she lifted her face to the bare ceiling above them. "But there's nay mistletoe about."

"Sure of that, are you?" Grinning, he reached up with one sinewy arm and plucked the sprig of greenery from his cap. Instead of his customary yew, the Fraser badge, the small yellowish flower and waxy white berries proclaimed it to be mistletoe. Holding it above her head, he fixed his gaze on hers, his expression softening. He tilted her face up to his. "Kiss me, my love, my lady, my Christmastide bride, for 'tis past midnight and now our wedding day. Mistletoe or no, I vow to make every day Christmas for us from this day forward."

Tears gathering, Alys opened her mouth to return the sentiment. Before she could, lips—warm, moist and mobile—covered hers, kissing her as she'd always dreamt of being kissed, only better. Large though he was, his hold was exquisitely gentle. He ran his big hands up and down her arms, smoothed his palms over the small of her back, and framed her waist as though she was some rare, cherished object he was afraid to break. Forgetting her fears, she tilted her head and parted her lips, then slid her tongue into his mouth, kissing him back with seven months of pent-up passion.

He slid a hand from her waist to her breast and groaned. "So beautiful, so verra beautiful." Cupping her, he flicked his thumb over her nipple, teasing it to life. Liquid heaviness settled between her thighs and with it a damp, drumming ache.

Alys arched against him. Melting like a snowflake brought indoors, reveling in the size and breadth and power of the male body molding to hers, she forgot everything save her desperate desire to join with him.

He drew away from her mouth and pressed fevered lips against her temple. "In but a few hours I will be your lord and master so far as the great wide world is concerned, but within these four chamber walls, it is I who am your vassal, your slave. And know this, lady, I mean to serve you well. There isna anything I wouldna do for you, no pleasure I would deny you." He let out a ragged breath and looked deeply into her eyes. "I would begin by giving you the first of your twelve Christmas gifts early. I would give you the first of those twelve great pleasures this verra moment."

He turned away from her to the small trestle table upon which the remains of her mostly untouched supper was set out. With the edge of his arm, he swept it clean, the trencher and empty goblet falling to the floor. He swung back to her, wrapped his arms about her, and lifted her atop it.

"My lord, it may be our wedding day but we're no yet married and the last time I—" Her voice broke off. How could she begin to explain the depth of her fears?

Setting her gently down, he shook his head, his eyes wearing a fevered, feral look. "A taste of forbidden fruit is allowed most betrothed couples. Had we chosen to be handfast wed, we'd have leave to enjoy the full orchard for a year and a day. If you do not believe me, I'll send for Father Fearghas to bear me out." He set a hand upon her knee, easing her legs apart.

"Callum Fraser, you'll do nay such thing!" She stopped when she realized he wasn't serious.

"Then I'll have to satisfy myself with kissing you. Only kisses, my sweetheart." Stepping between her splayed thighs, he feathered his lips over hers. Alys moaned, feeling each sweep of his mouth like fire. "Just kisses." He touched his lips to hers again, more firmly this time. "Once we are wed on the morrow, I will consecrate my body to your pleasure for the rest of our earthly days—and nights."

Alys could resist no more. She held his lean,

handsome face between her hands and opened for him like a flower. "Oh, my lord, my sweet lord."

His tongue entered her, as wickedly delicious and insistent as the rest of him. And suddenly Alys was hungry, ravenous, more starved than she could ever recall being. Never before had she felt such need, known such want. The light kiss burst into a sparring match of tangling tongues and nipping teeth. Caught up in the midnight madness, she felt almost a virgin again. Whatever whore's tricks she'd performed in the past, whatever passion her former husband had coaxed from her girlish body were forgotten. She was Callum Fraser's lady and with his touch, he was washing her clean.

He broke contact with her lips to lay a trail of damp, biting kisses at the sensitive spot behind her ear, the line of her throat leading into the curve of her shoulder, the tips of her breasts, first laving her through the thin fabric, then pushing one sleeve off her shoulder and down.

He breathed against her breast. "Ah, you're all roses here, too."

She sobbed and tried pulling back but Callum wouldn't allow it. Gently but firmly he held her in place. "Just kisses, my lady, only kisses."

Dragging her nipple into his mouth, he tugged, he suckled, he pleased. Blessed wetness trickled between her legs. The tingling throttled to full-scale throbbing. He ran his hands, so warm, so strong, so knowing, along her legs from ankle to thigh, carrying the hem of her shift upwards to her waist. Cool air brushed her inner thighs, raising gooseflesh.

Fear shot through her. She was about to break her

vow, jeopardize their love, wreak havoc upon their future… With weak arms, she managed to shove against his chest. "My lord, you break your word to me. Only kisses, just kisses, you promised."

He slipped his hand between her legs and found her with his finger. "There are many kinds of kisses, twelve at least, and each night I mean to show you a different one."

He was too strong for her, too wickedly persuasive, too skilled in the loving arts. She sagged against him, her hands sliding into the silk of his hair, her thighs trembling with the force of her need.

Gently he worked the furled flesh, spreading her between his big blunt fingers, coaxing her to new levels of desperate, aching desire. Holding her open, he stepped back and stared hungrily at her most private spot.

"Just kisses, only kisses, I swear it to you. Let these be the first of twelve nights of wicked wedding gifts we shall share."

He knelt on one knee before her, his head level with her splayed thighs. Disappearing between them, he found her with his mouth. Alys moaned. Never before had a man "kissed" her there, not even Alex. Callum must have done this before, though, for he was very, very good. He swirled his tongue in a most wondrous way, unlocking some secret, private part. Time, which had seemed so monumentally important earlier, spiraled to a standstill. It was finally Christmas, their wedding day, and they seemed to have all the time in the world.

Pleasure poured over her, wave upon wave, carrying her higher toward some as yet unknown crest. Thighs aquiver, she anchored her hands to the shelf of Callum's beautiful shoulders and lifted herself to his plundering mouth.

He brushed his rough cheek along the insides of her thighs and looked up at her with shining eyes. "Your inner lips are a darker, duskier pink than your mouth and your nectar even more juicy sweet. Tomorrow night, I will kiss you thus again only when I do you will straddle my face and ride my mouth and take your pleasure again and again until you can take no more."

Never before had a man said such deliciously wicked things to her, let alone done them. But as wicked as Callum was, he was even more generous. He wanted to please her, he was determined to please her, and she was coming to see that his own pleasure depended upon hers.

Alys sighed. Whatever suffering she'd endured, it had brought her to this amazing man, and she regretted it not. She was a most fortunate woman, and she meant to stay so.

"Mind your promise, my lord, only kisses—and such wondrous lovely kisses they are, I would have more of them."

She slid her hand to the back of his head, drawing him closer, drawing him down. He reached her, his mouth spanning her, his tongue sliding along the seam between her nether lips.

Alys gasped. "Sweet, my lord!"

She could feel herself running into his mouth like a river and feel him just as greedily lapping her up. He licked at her labia as though it were a summertime fruit of which he couldn't possibly get enough and then found the core of her with what must be the very tip of his tongue. Alys gasped again. A raw sob ripped forth from her throat. So much kindness, so much pleasure and all of it focused on her. Never before had she felt so enormously special, so completely and unconditionally loved. How could she possibly bear it?

"Easy, my love." Callum ran his beard-roughened cheek along her leg, his gaze catching at hers. "I will give you all the kisses you desire and more. Only lean back, my dearling, and give me leave to show you just what a good husband I mean to be."

She did as he bid, letting the cleansing pleasure wash over her, *through* her. For now she refused to think of old wives and their warnings, refused to believe that sharing love such as this could be anything other than true and right.

The culmination struck with the fury of a storm at sea. Had she been standing, the force of it would have knocked her to her knees. Like a thunderbolt ripping through a placid summer sky, there was no warning, no time to prepare. Suddenly it was upon her, she was in it, and there was no recourse but to ride out its rage. Pleasure crashed over her, through her. It eddied. It pooled. It rose in cresting waves and dipped in dizzying spirals. Cast adrift upon a tumult-tossed loch, captured in a tiny boat she'd no hope of steering, she could do no more than hold on and pray for calmer waters to once more prevail.

"Merry Christmas, wife."

Alys opened her eyes. She looked down into her soon-to-be bridegroom's stark gaze and dazzling smile. His forehead was damp from the exertion of loving her, his lips shiny and ever so slightly swollen. Like fitting together a tavern puzzle, she pieced together the sights and sensations to form the full picture of where she was and exactly what she'd just allowed. Her shift rode her waist. Her bare legs were open. Her pubis was exposed, her womanhood pulsing with the ghost of an unholy heat. Liquid warmth leaked along one inner thigh. The scent and heat of her satisfaction rose between them like a spiral of steam. Nor was she alone affected. The swollen ridge tenting the front of Callum's kilt told her he was heavily aroused, swollen to bursting with unsatisfied need, and yet he made no move to press for more. Only kisses, he'd sworn to her, and even those he'd selflessly given, taking nothing for himself. Whatever fears she'd held on to that he might be marrying her for less than love, she released now. He wanted her, he lusted for her, but beyond that, he loved her, loved her true. Emotion overcame her. Tears touched her lashes, her cheeks, and then slid down to her jaw. She was weeping on Christmas Day, her wedding day, and she couldn't seem to find the will to stop.

Gently, very gently, Callum pulled down her shift. "Sweetheart, I meant to make you smile, not cry."

"I know. And I am smiling, albeit on the inside." She shook her head, dashing away the wetness. "'Tis only I'd nay notion...*kissing* could be so wondrous."

In her innocence, she'd thought Alex a tender and generous lover, but she understood she'd never before been on the receiving end of a man's selfless generosity, his unbridled tenderness. Not only had she never before reached the pinnacle of pleasure, but ere tonight, she'd no notion that such a summit even existed. She wished she might be as clever with words as she was with her sewing needle so that she might give voice to the feelings flooding her heart. But eloquence was the gift of her friend, Brianna. Alys was but a simple maid.

And so she settled on the only two words that came to mind, simple words and yet she hoped her gaze and touch would suffice to send them soaring. "Thank you." She ran her hands over his chest, the coarse matting of dark hair showing through the saffron linen, and laid fervent kisses along his muscle-corded neck.

He exhaled heavily and stood. Even though they'd broken contact, she could still feel the tension bunching his muscles. It was costing him a great deal to keep his word and walk away, and yet she'd no doubt that walk away he would. Not because loving her had made him a good man or a better man or indeed had changed him in any appreciable way, but because he loved her, he truly loved her. For Alys, that wasn't simply good enough. It was everything.

"That was but a taste of forbidden fruit. Tomorrow night, once our vows are said and our guests well met, I mean to devour the dish entire."

The passion she'd just experienced had stripped her bare, rubbed her raw. There was no more room for dissembling. From here on, she could give him nothing but the absolute truth, no matter how ugly and disastrous that truth might prove.

"There is something more you should know about me." The admission sapped what little courage she had managed to muster.

She tried ducking away, but Callum would have none of it. He cupped her chin in his hand and lifted her face to look up at him. "What is it, love? What troubles weigh so heavy upon these slight shoulders? Tell me, Alys, so that I can make whatever it is disappear."

Even now, the force of his love humbled her. These seven months he had sworn to be a better man for her, but it was she who must strive to be better for him. "You have already been so good to us, Alasdair and me. You have given us so much, too much, I think."

"To give you too much would be impossible." His deep blue gaze locked upon hers and he shook his head. Mayhap it was a trick of the flickering light but his eyes looked damp. "For you, lady, I would slay dragons."

Shamed by his steadfastness, she dropped her gaze, cursing herself for her cowardice all these many months. "When Alasdair was born, there were…difficulties. I am…small and he was big even as a newborn. The midwife warned I might not be able to conceive another child." The secret, her last, had weighed heavy upon her since she'd accepted his suit but never more so than this moment.

His falling face confirmed he hadn't expected that. "I see."

Alys hugged herself hard. Why, oh why, was she destined to disappoint the men who loved her? First her father and then Alex and now Callum—and Callum's disappointment was the hardest to bear of all because she loved him the most. Her heart, which only minutes ago had soared like an eagle, fell to the floor like a bird on the receiving end of a hunter's arrow.

She reached out and laid a hand on his forearm, steely strong like the rest of him. "I would have told you ere now, only I couldna bear to think of losing you. But it isna too late. Let us be handfast wed instead. If after a year and a day, I havena conceived, you can cast me off and wed a lady worthy of you."

Callum's eyes widened. If he'd seemed shocked a moment ago, he appeared doubly so now. "Cast you off! I'd sooner sever my arm than lose you."

Alys sighed. He was so very dear to her, so very good and true for all his former roguish ways. "You say that now, my lord, but you may feel differently in time. I have a child already. I have Alasdair. If need be, he will be enough. He *is* enough. But you, my dearest lord, have no child. You canna ken the great joy you'd be forsaking if we're no blessed with children."

His expression softened. His gaze melted. He tucked a stray curl behind her ear, his glancing touch gentle beyond words, even simple ones. "I willna lie to you, sweetheart. If we do not have bairns, I will be disappointed, saddened even. But if I do not have you, I will be lost."

Fresh tears filled her eyes, tears of relief and gratitude. Not many men would be willing to take a possibly barren wife to their bosom. "You are resolved, then?"

He nodded fiercely. "Come what may, I dinna desire to marry you for a year and a day but for the rest of our earthly lives."

"Oh, Callum, you truly are so verra good to me."

He wrapped his arms about her and tucked her head beneath his chin. "I am nay good by nature but you make me want to be good, Alys, or at least as good as I may be."

"Oh, Callum, you are good, the very best of men." She hugged him back, drawing strength from his solid warmth, his unwavering love. Unlike her first husband, Callum wasn't going to leave her, not for a whim, not for any reason.

He stepped back. Smiling, he shook his head. "So 'tis true, then. Love really is blind."

She smacked his shoulder. "My eyes are in fine working order, and I tell you that you, Callum Fraser, are a good man."

Callum was such a wondrous lovely man. It hurt her heart sometimes to see what a poor opinion he had of himself, how he turned a blind eye to his own fine qualities. He seemed to forgive everyone's faults but his. Frequently he compared himself to his twin, Ewan, and just as frequently, he found himself failing. Brianna's husband was a fine man, and he loved her friend with the whole of his heart. Still, in Alys's experience, sinners tended to be far more tolerant than saints. She doubted Lord Ewan would have been as accepting of her past as was her soon-to-be lord.

She reached up and traced the sharp blade of his cheekbone with a single finger. "You're no saint, I'll grant you that. But then, who's to say the saints themselves were all so verra saintly? I can't help but think they must have had their failings, too. You, at least, own yours honestly."

The smile he beamed would have stolen her heart had he not owned it already. "Small wonder I want to be a better man for you. How could I not, when you always see the verra best in me." He leaned in. Anticipating his kiss, Alys let her eyes drift closed.

"Och!"

Callum's deep grunt, of pain not pleasure, had her opening her eyes. She reached for him but too late. He staggered and fell back, striking the floor.

2

SQUINTING THROUGH the canopy of shooting stars, Callum made out Milread standing over him, broom held high. "Have you gone soft in the head, Callum Fraser, to come to your bride's chamber on the eve of your wedding and disport yourself as though you were wedded already? You're nay supposed to so much as set eyes upon her let alone do—" she waved a clawlike hand to indicate the overturned trencher, goblets and scattered cutlery "—*that!*"

Holding a hand to his pounding skull, Callum clamored to his feet. To find himself felled by a wee witch woman who scarcely came up to his waist would be a mighty blow to any man's pride—but before his bride, no less!

He wheeled on her. "A curse on you, crone. I would have your head on a pike were you not my sister-in-law's creature."

"And my dear friend, as well," Alys chimed in, stepping swiftly between them. She leaned into Callum and peered up at him. "How fares your head, my lord? You seem a wee bit flushed."

"I'm fine!" he snapped, though judging from the throbbing, the assault had raised a goodly sized knot.

Milread rolled her crooked shoulders and spat upon his boot tops. "Fie, he's a Fraser, isna he? They come with verra hard heads."

"Why you—"

Callum's code of conduct wouldn't permit him to strike a woman, no matter how irritating that woman might be. So he did the next best thing, raising his fist high and punching air instead.

Alys moved to block Milread with her body. She wasn't a tall woman but still she topped the crone by a full head. "Pray let us not argue and on Christmas, nay less." She cast Callum a pointed look. "She means only to guard us against ill-luck."

He peered around her to look at Milread, the devil's own grin splitting her wrinkled face. "Guard us, that one! She'll lead us straight to Hell more like. She's no guardian angel but one of Beelzebub's fiends."

Milread ducked beneath Alys's raised arm. "Mayhap I am, for 'tis fiendish delight I take in sending you off with that mighty pike in your pants." She poked her stick at the bulge still throbbing between his thighs.

Cupping himself, Callum backed up lest a knot on his noggin be the least of the Christmas "gifts" the crone gave him. "Why, I'd as soon shove a pike down your gullet as—"

"Soft now, my lad, that great staff of yours shall find relief soon enough." Aiming her weapon, Milread advanced. "For now, away with you and leave my lady to her rest."

Alys blew him a kiss as he backed toward the door. Reaching behind him, he found the handle and turned it. "I will do as you bid, witch, but mind your mistress sleeps well, for she'll have little enough rest tomorrow night or the other eleven to follow."

CALLUM SLAMMED the door behind him, sending the candles sputtering in their sconces.

Alys turned back to Milread and sighed. "Milread, truly, that was very bad of you."

The crone answered her with a dismissive wave. "Och, 'tis his pride that's hurting more than his head. To think all my safekeeping's been undone by that one's selfishness. I will offer up a sacrifice to Lord Odin first thing on the morrow." Broom in hand, she shuffled through the rushes to where the scattered supper lay.

Contrite, Alys followed her. "Let me do that."

Scowling, Milread shooed her away. "To bed with you."

Lest she give further offense, Alys obeyed.

Sweeping the spillage into a pile, Milread chortled. "Your lord's head isna the only part of him that's hard." Leaning folded hands atop the broom handle, she turned toward her charge and cackled. "Randy as a bull your bridegroom is."

Alys climbed into bed. "Aye, he is." If tonight's "kissing" was any sign, their wedding night promised to be merry and memorable indeed.

Wishing she were inclined to sleep, she sat cross-legged at the foot of the bed, idly stroking the beard burn branding her cheek. Minded of all the ways her lord had loved her—kisses, only kisses—had her womanhood beating like a tiny heart.

"How did you find Alasdair?" Guiltily she realized

that she'd been too caught up with Callum and her own pleasure to spare her son so much as a thought.

Milread looked up from the pile she was creating and beamed. She was very fond of babies, but Alasdair especially. "Sleeping like a wee lamb, snuggled up to that stray you found for him."

Alys smiled, too. The past summer she'd saved Cat from drowning at the hands of Callum's cook—*former* cook. His "crime" had been to lick a joint of beef that had been left sitting out. Alys well remembered her "hungry days" in the months bracketing Alasdair's birth, as well as what it felt like to bear the brunt of injustice. She'd scooped up the tabby and taken him under her care. Cat and Alasdair had become fast friends. Upon introducing the two, she'd shown her son how to approach and stroke Cat so that the animal would not be spooked nor Alasdair scratched. Even though he was a baby still, Alasdair was very gentle and Cat responded in kind.

Thinking of how adorable they were together, Alys felt her smile broadening. "I'd say Cat is stray nay more. Alasdair loves him dearly and even Callum tolerates him." She'd even caught him feeding the cat scraps a time or two when he thought no one was watching.

Milread nodded. "It is good for a child to have a pet. There is much to be learned from tending creatures who dinna speak with words." Her task complete, she propped the broom in the corner. "Mayhap next time this year you'll give him another friend, a two-legged one, a wee brother or sister to bear him company."

Alys felt her spirits dip. She wanted Callum's baby

with all her heart. For the second time that night, the midwife's warning came back to haunt her.

"I hope so. Otherwise Alasdair is in danger of becoming more spoiled still. And Callum would make the best of fathers. I see him with Alasdair and…" Alys ended the thought there, pulled over one of the banked pillows, and hugged it to her breast. "I know my lord is a hard man and as unlike his brother as night is to day, and yet with us he is gentle as a lamb and so…wonderfully tender."

Milread snorted. "Wheesht, lassie, pray to the gods you think the same of him a year hence."

Come what may, I dinna desire to marry you for a year and a day but for the rest of our earthly lives.

Alys sighed. She lifted a hand and absently traced the outline of her sensitized lower lip. "I will, Milread. I know I will."

Certain as she was of Callum, she was still uncertain of what the future might hold. She'd learned not to trust happiness. Just after she and Alexander had married, he'd announced he was rejoining his English knight's army. She'd pleaded and argued with him, to no avail. He'd been adamant. This stubbornness was a side of him she'd never before seen. But he'd been tender, too, swearing to return for the birthing. As much as she'd wanted to believe him, in her heart she'd known his parting kiss would be their last, that the child growing inside her would know no parent save her. When the letter informing her of his death finally found its way to her, read aloud by a kindly priest from the Church of St. Andrew, she'd dropped to her knees, devastated but not really surprised.

Callum's coming into her life had brought her joy such as she'd never before known. The past seven months' courtship still seemed more fairy tale than reality. Even the antipathy between him and her best friend, Brianna, had been laid to rest upon Brianna and Ewan's marriage last spring. Her best friend and the love of her life were allies once more, which gladdened her heart greatly.

And yet on the eve of her own Christmas wedding, she couldn't entirely trust her good fortune. She thought of the lifetime of companionable days and delicious nights that lay ahead, the lifetime of unending Christmas Callum swore to give her, and clutched the pillow tighter. Perfect happiness was within her grasp. Given her history, could she hope to hold on to it?

Sightless though she was, the old woman seemed to be studying her intently. "Something's amiss, child. Tell me what troubles you?"

At a loss for words, Alys shook her head. Tears welled. Her shoulders shook. She bowed her head. "I never thought to be anyone's bride again."

Having trod the prostitute's path, she'd never expected any man to want her for more than his mistress. And yet Callum knew of he past and still he wanted her for his wife. The seven months' waiting she'd imposed had only strengthened his resolve.

"Och, dinna fret so!" Milread shuffled through the rushes toward her and enfolded Alys in bony but loving arms. "Life often brings to us gifts that we least expect."

Alys shook her head. "You ken my past. I canna come to my husband as a virgin and yet when I am with him, I feel as if the world was fresh and new and I a maid once more."

Milread laid her gnarled hand atop Alys's and gave it a wee pat. "Loving another with all one's being has washed many a soiled soul clean. And your bridegroom is nay saint himself. Be bold and buxom in bed tomorrow night, wean, and you'll find the Fraser well-pleased with his bride. Once you are his lady in every sense, passion's fire will burn away these dark doubts and misgivings from your mind."

Alys looked up. "Do you really believe so?"

Milread snorted. "Barring Lord Ewan, I've never set eyes upon a man so besotted with his bride." She framed Alys's face in her clawlike hands. "Now tell me, what can I do to bring a smile to that bonny face?"

Alys hesitated. The terrible foreboding that had taken hold of her upon waking that morning had grown steadily stronger throughout the day. Now that Callum was gone, she felt as though a brigade of bogeymen might be coming for her at any time.

Unused to asking for what she wanted, she said, "Well, there is one thing…"

"Name it, child, and I will do my best to make it so."

She slipped her gaze to the cord at Milread's waist from which a faded crimson pouch swung. "I crave the boon of your soothsaying. Will you read the runes for me?"

Milread waved a hand in the air. "Bah, those old stones are best kept in their pouch. The Fraser loves you true, lassie. I've no need of runes to tell that."

Suddenly desperate, Alys caught at her hand. "But the stones can be used to answer other kinds of questions, can they not? Will I be able to give him a child? Will he still come to my bed when I'm old and gray? Will we live long and happy?"

Milread released a put-upon sigh. "Sometimes it is wiser not to ken the future. Both joy and sorrow are best met in the moment."

"Milread, please, all day I have fretted and worried."

The crone blew out a breath and loosened the cord of her pouch. She drew out a balled white cloth, shook it out, and spread it upon the foot of the bed, then handed the bag to Alys. "There are twenty-five stones in that bag, twenty-four bearing the sacred Norse symbols and one left blank. Shake the bag well, slip your hand inside and knead the stones so that they absorb your energy."

At Milread's direction, Alys stood at the southern edge of the bed, held the runes betwixt her hands, and silently asked her question. *What does the future hold for my marriage to Callum?*

"When you feel ready, let the runes tumble out onto the coverlet," Milread instructed.

Alys nodded, drew a deep breath, and released them.

"Good, good." Milread came around and turned the stones with symbols showing facedown. "Now with your eyes closed, pass your right hand over the pieces. Quiet your mind and let your hands feel the energy of the stones as they speak to you."

Alys did as Milread bade her. She felt coldness creep into her palm when she passed over some pieces, warmth when passing over others. For both extremes, she experienced a definite tingling.

"When you are ready, open your eyes and choose seven stones, nay more, nay less, and lay each down in order."

Alys chose seven stones in turn, having a care to keep them facedown for now.

When she'd finished, Milread turned them faceup. The vertical cuts meant nothing to Alys, but they obviously meant a great deal to Milread. The crone's wrinkled face had turned ashen, her sightless eyes saucer wide and staring.

Alys leaned in for a look. "What is it? What do you see?"

Milread's milky gaze shuttered. "I see nothing." She snatched up the stones and shoved them back in the bag.

Alys grabbed at the old woman's arm. "I don't believe you. You always see something. I know you foretold Brianna's and Ewan's marriage."

Milread blew out a breath. "My lady and Lord Ewan plighted their troth as weans. The taking of a blood oath as good as set the outcome in stone."

Alys refused to be put off. "Tell me what you see. Please, Milread, I need to know. You look as though you've seen a specter. You're trembling."

Milread shook her head, fiercely this time, the grizzled strands lashing at her face. "I am old, child, and the cold coming through the cracks in the casement makes my bones ache and my limbs tremble. That is all."

Alys drew back. "You are certain there is nothing amiss?" As much as she wished to believe her friend, the hairs standing at attention on her nape and the chill settling over the rest of her told her she should not.

"Aye, I am. The runes give a jumbled message,

most likely because both of us are spent. Now leave off your worrying and climb back into bed. You'll want a bonny face to show your lord upon the morrow. And for that, even one as young and fair as you must have rest."

Alys nodded. "If you are sure…"

Instinct told her that Milread was holding something back. Whatever that something was, the firm press of the crone's shrunken lips also told her she'd receive no satisfaction this night. She was beginning to think she'd get no sleep, as well.

Milread spoke up. "Rune reading is thirsty work. Let us drink to Christmas and weddings and happy times."

Alys nodded. She wasn't particularly thirsty, but mayhap the wine would calm her nerves and still her racing thoughts.

Milread crossed the room to the trestle table. Fortunately the earlier passionate interlude had not resulted in the flagon being upturned, only the empty goblets. Turning her humped back to Alys, she poured out the wine.

She turned about, retraced her path to the bed, and handed one of the goblets to Alys. Raising her own cup high, she proclaimed, "May the gods bless and mind you all your days."

Alys touched her goblet to Milread's. "Merry Christmas, Milread." She took a small sip.

The wine, she thought, had a very queer tang. She wondered if it might be bad though the half-cup she'd had earlier in the night had tasted fine.

Milread drained hers in a single swallow. She wiped her mouth on the wrinkled back of one liver-spotted hand and regarded Alys's still full cup with an assessing eye. "Drink it down, lass."

Not wanting to seem ungrateful, Alys did as Milread asked. Licking the sourness from her lips, she handed over her empty cup and crawled beneath the turned-down coverlet.

Milread pulled it up over her. Alys reached out and clasped the small, roughened hands. "I am sorry Brie canna come, but I'm so verra glad she sent you in her stead."

Seven months gone with her first babe, Brianna was too big for travel even by litter, and her husband, Lord Ewan, far too devoted to leave her side even for his brother's wedding. As much as Alys missed having her best friend with her, she would not have Brianna take any risks for her sake.

Milread's rheumy eyes misted. "Wheesht, child, it will be some years yet afore I am food for the crows. Until then I mean to make as merry as I may. I wouldna miss your wedding for all the world's treasures."

Alys yawned and burrowed beneath the bedding, a lovely, unexpected relaxation slipping over her. "Do you really have an extra eye, Milread?"

Milread nodded and pulled the coverlet up. "Aye, child, I do but then so do we all. The Third Eye sets betwixt our two seen eyes albeit ever so slightly above. It opens when we have need of seeing the inner truth of people and things. Because of my blindness, I've learnt to keep mine open always, even whilst I sleep."

Suddenly Alys could scarcely hold her eyes open. Yawning, again, she snuggled onto her side. Mere moments ago she'd been worrying about something, but for the life of her, she couldn't remember what.

"Good night, child." Milread's voice seemed to float above her like a protective cloud. "May Odin and Frigga bring you sweet dreams."

ALYS DIDN'T ANSWER. Milread stared down at her charge. The girl's aura was rosebud pink and glowing gold except for one gash of crimson, the mark of a not yet fully healed psychic wound; otherwise she was the picture of peace. Her soft, rhythmic breathing announced the sleeping draught had done its swift work. She slept. Her slumber would be both dreamless and deeply restful, which was just as well, for she would need all her strength in both mind and body for the trial that awaited her.

Milread turned away from the bed. Pacing the chamber, she hadn't felt so helpless since seven months before, when Brianna had set out to rescue Lord Ewan, taking only Alys with her. The two young women had very nearly met their deaths at the hand of the villainous Duncan. Fortunately, Ewan had broken free of his captors and circled back with Callum. It had been Callum's arrow that had felled Duncan, saving all three lives.

But events couldn't always be counted upon to work out so neatly. At times everyone needed a little magick, a celestial helping hand. Spent from worry, Mildread curled up on the pallet at the foot of the bed. A shudder ran through her, wracking her bones like a great gale. Alys had spoken true. The runes had been both deeply telling and frighteningly dire.

THURISAZ, which suggested the present run of bonny fortune was about to end.

ANSUZ reversed—trickery, lies, deceit.

WYRD—the abyss, a void of all hope.

NIED—a time of extreme emotional travail, crossing the abyss.

PERDHRO—a dark secret about to come to light. Alys's prostitute past leapt to mind and settled there. By all the gods, Milread prayed not. The poor child had suffered more than sufficient on that score.

WUNJO, reversed, a crisis, most especially love reversed. If Callum Fraser forsook her lady, by God she'd see his cods cut off!

And lastly HAGALL, hail, foretelling of calamitous natural events, in the main…

Death.

STALKING DOWN THE CORRIDOR to his solar, Callum allowed that while seven months of celibacy may have improved the state of his soul, it had little benefited his sense of humor. Head aching and balls hard, he marveled at his uncommon restraint. Even as a beardless youth, he'd been intensely sexual, and the females in his orbit had responded in kind. Like ripe apples, willing women had been falling into his lap since he'd bedded his first wench at the age of thirteen. Committing himself to any one woman had been a concept beyond his ken.

But Alys was different. Alys was his true love. He'd known it from the day she'd happened upon him sitting amongst the weeds in his mother's abandoned garden.

He still marveled at how her quiet presence had lit up that sad, shadowed little corner like a sunbeam. The moment she'd wandered inside, all big blue eyes and shy smiles, the scraggly shrubs had seemed to spring to life, to bear blooms the very pale pink of her perfect rosebud lips.

Given his past paramours, it wasn't fair of him to begrudge Alys her one lost love, a dead husband no less, and yet he did, God how he did. Alex Field— Callum hated the Englishman, the Outlander, with the whole of his hypocritical heart. He was jealous of a dead man. It was madness, and yet he couldn't help himself. Admittedly it wasn't fair to condemn a man he'd never met, yet from the little he knew of Alys's first marriage, he'd pegged Alexander Field as a codless scut. Like sour wine, a man leaving his pregnant wife alone in a foreign city with no family or friends left a bad taste in his mouth.

Fortunately his ill feelings didn't extend to the boy, Alasdair. He'd first reached out to the child for Alys's sake, but in the seven months since, he'd grown to love the lad for himself. He was a bonny boy, sweet-natured like his mother, and in spite of all the love she lavished upon him, sadly starved for male attention. Callum couldn't make him his heir, but he meant to be a father to him in every other way.

He entered his solar with relief. As he did, he realized this was the last time he would cross his threshold as a bachelor. That thought brought relief and a sense of peace, not the panic he once would have felt. He couldn't wait to make Alys his bride in truth, to bring her back to his chamber, and aye, his bed. Closing the door behind him, he began shucking off his clothes. With luck his dreams would afford him the sweet relief of finishing what he'd started in Alys's chamber.

Naked and painfully aroused, he crossed the chamber to the bed. Eager to plunge beneath the coverlet and sate himself in sleep, he brushed the bed hangings aside.

"What mischief making is this?"

He stared down, scarcely able to credit the proof of his eyes. Rose petals, hundreds, nay thousands, formed a fragrant pink carpet across his coverlet. The willow branch lying across the banked pillows was the settling of it. Milread! Cupid's culprit was none other than Brianna's crone. The witch had invaded his sanctum and still had managed to return to Alys's chamber in time to spoil his sport. Scattering rosebuds was all well and good but where the devil was he supposed to sleep?

Fury lanced through him. A man's castle was supposed to be just that. He swung back his arm, intending to sweep the bed clear, and then stalled himself. The petals reminded him of Alys's rosebud lips. He picked one up and rubbed it betwixt his thumb and forefinger, testing its texture. Soft, so very soft. The troubadour's tributes didn't lie. His lady's rosebud mouth truly was petal-soft and her skin, too. From the glimpse he'd gotten through her nightgown, tight pink rosebuds tipped her lovely breasts, as well. And her heart was the softest part of her. If ever a woman deserved to be loved upon a bower of roses, it was his lady.

He turned away from the bed and walked over to the cupboard. Pulling on his cloak, he settled himself into a brocade-covered chair by the fire. As a boy he'd made it a custom to stay awake on Christmastide Eve. Even after wrapping and rewrapping his purloined presents, still he'd been too excited to sleep. "Callum's Christmastide Vigil" his parents had called it.

He held the petal to his nose, inhaling its fragrance. Dawn was mere hours away. Christmas came but once a year, a wedding but once in a man's life. He had the rest of his life to sleep.

He'd broken enough traditions for one night.

3

CHRISTMAS MORN DAWNED clear and bright. Everyone, Alys included, agreed no winter bride could call for a bonnier wedding day. And yet despite awaking from a deeply restful and strangely dreamless sleep, the previous day's misgivings returned the moment her feet touched upon the floor. Milread had seen something in that rune cast, something evil and dark. If Alys had doubted it before, the witch woman's uncommon quietude whilst helping her dress was the settling of it. But no amount of persuasion could coax the old woman to say aught on the matter.

The nuptials took place in the Fraser chapel, the railed altar festooned with holly and yew and delicate white snowdrops known also as Candle Mass Bells. Callum's household priest and former tutor, Father Fearghas officiated the ceremony and subsequent mass. Owing to her prostitute's past, Alys often felt anxious with clergymen, but the rotund little priest with his twinkling eyes and easy smile instantly set her at ease.

Still when the good father came to the passage in the ceremony where he asked the congregants if they knew of any reason why she and Callum should not be joined, Alys held her breath. Beyond Brianna, Ewan, Milread and of course Callum, her past was a secret she hoped to carry with her to the grave.

Her fear must have shown on her face. Squeezing her hand, Callum leaned in and whispered, "Dinna fret, dearling. If anyone speaks up, I'll run him through."

He punctuated the promise with a wink and a smile and a touch to the dagger at his waist. Improbably Alys found herself smiling, too.

The moment passed. Save for an errant cough and shuffling foot, the chapel stayed silent and still. They repeated their vows in turn, swearing to love, honor and cherish each other all their days. Some erstwhile bachelors might demonstrate hesitancy when faced with changing their state, but not Callum. He spoke his promises in a deep, sure voice that resonated within the chapel and within Alys's heart.

When her turn came, she looked up into her laird's deep blue eyes, fringed with lovely long jet lashes, saw the love he held for her there, and said the sacred words from the wellspring of gladness flooding her heart. That her version of the vow included a promise to be "bold and buxom in bed" had her blood heating and her heart quickening.

Afterward, Father Fearghas bade her hold out her hand. Callum slid his ancestral ruby ring upon her finger, the sealing to her happiness. Turning her hand over and resting it in his, he leaned down and kissed her palm before repeating:

"With this ring I thee wed,

This gold and silver I thee give,
With my body I thee worship,
And with this dowry I thee endow."

Dividing his beaming gaze between them, Father Fearghas declared, "With the power vested in me by God the Father Almighty and the Holy Church, I now pronounce you man and wife. Go with God, my children, and may you find Christmas in each other for as long as you both shall live." He turned his round, plain face to Callum and broke into a broad grin. "What are you waiting on, lad? Kiss your bride."

Callum winked. "This part, Father, I can well manage without divine direction or yours." Grinning, he spared the priest a swift sideways glance and then turned to Alys. "Come to me, my lady, my wife." Before she could take so much as a step toward him, he opened his arms and enfolded her in a hearty embrace.

Like a snowflake exposed to a blazing fire, Alys felt herself melting into him. Their mouths met, their souls melded. They'd kissed many times before, but this time was different, sanctified and sacred.

Against her mouth, Callum whispered, "Flesh of my flesh, heart of my heart…" His tongue swept the seam of her lips and she opened for him without hesitancy, taking his breath into her body and his love into her heart.

It took the good father prying them apart to call them back to the fact that they were in public and in a sanctuary, no less. Planting a palm on Callum's shoulder, he shook his head and whispered, "Wheesht, lad, cool your cods whilst in my chapel. The bedding will come anon."

Laughing, they turned to greet their guests. Standing

behind, Father Fearghas laid a hand on either of their shoulders. "Gentle folk, I give you Callum, Laird of the Frasers and his wife, the Lady Alys."

Wild clapping ensued. Looking down onto the congregants standing behind the rail, Alys saw Milread dashing what surely must be a tear from her eye. Propped upon the rail, Alasdair waived with both arms, his wee body wrapped in a tiny Fraser plaid.

Callum brushed his lip against her ear. "Come, my lady, let us collect our son so that we may celebrate Christmas as a family."

Alys shot up her head. "*Our* son?"

His smile broadened. "Aye, yours, mine, and nay other's." He held onto her hand and together they descended the stone steps.

Coming upon them, Callum fixed his gaze upon the crone. "So witch, have you nay curses or blows for me today?"

Milread snorted but her milky eyes remained misty. "As husbands come, you might just do."

Callum tossed back his head and laughed. "Coming from you, 'tis high praise indeed."

He reached out and took Alasdair from her. Cooing with delight, the babe threw his chubby arms about Callum's neck. "Papa, Papa, come!"

Alys felt her full heart fisting. She stroked a hand over Alasdair's downy curls and brushed a kiss on Callum's lean cheek. Things were going to be all right. They *were* all right. Her true love stood beside her, now her lawful lord. She felt the weight of his ruby ring upon her finger and the force of his love in the deep blue gaze he fixed upon her. Her dear little Alasdair was nestled between them, happier than he'd ever before seemed. For the first time since Alex had persuaded her to run off with him, she felt as if she was part of a family. She felt as if she was at long last home.

They headed the processional across the courtyard to the great hall, Alasdair riding Callum's shoulders and Alys walking beside them holding her lord's hand. Stepping inside, she felt as though she'd entered a Christmas fairyland. Bows of evergreen laced with holly, ivy and mistletoe hung from the timber-beamed ceiling, their pungency filling the hall. Sprays of snowdrops, the special flowers of Christmas, took pride of place in the center of each of the dozen odd trestle tables. Savory scents greeted them. Wassail and hot pasty pies were already making the rounds. Callum's cooks had scarcely seen daylight for three days, working into the wee hours preparing delicacies both savory and sweet. Platter upon platter of fine fare was being carried inside from the kitchen. Roasted quail, goose, venison, boar, mutton, salted salmon and smoked oysters, great wheels of cheeses, and any number of breads and tarts and custards would grace the groaning boards this first day of Christmas throughout Twelfth Night.

From the screened minstrel's gallery above bagpipes played. Within the massive fireplace, in lieu of the usual peat fire, a great Yule log crackled and burned. A dais draped in the Fraser colors stood beneath a massive tapestry depicting the clan's coat of arms.

Callum handed Alasdair off to Milread and offered Alys his arm. "My lady, will you do me the honor of dining by my side?"

Alys didn't hesitate. This was her day, *their* day, and she swore to be done with shame and shyness.

She laid her arm atop the hard shelf of his forearm. "My lord, your side is the only place I shall ever again desire to be."

He bent low to her ear. "Then let us feast with these fools a whit and then we will retire to our bridal bower. There lady, we shall dine on the ambrosia of one another's bodies like gods."

He led her up the three short steps to their places at the head table. Standing atop, she felt as though she was living a dream, a fairy tale.

She turned to Callum. "My lord, it is all too perfect."

He lifted the chased silver bride cup and directed his powerful voice out onto the standing assembly of their kinfolk and company. "Gentle folk, I bid you a merry First Day of Christmas and present to you my bonny bride, the Lady Alys. I command you, good masters and mistresses, to love and honor this lady as I do, for from this day forth she is my helpmate and consort, the mother of my future sons and daughters, and above all, my most beloved wife."

Shouts of "huzzah" rose about the hall, the vibrations reaching to the rafters. More toasts were made and drunk, most extolling the beauty, virtue, and goodness of the bride. Though Alys had tended toward shyness all her life, looking out onto the assembly of well-wishers, she made a point of holding her head high and her back straight. This was her first official feast day as Callum's lady wife, and she wanted her lord to be proud of her.

And so he seemed to be. Smiling, Callum offered her

the goblet, pressing the rim to her lower lip. She took a sip and passed it back, holding the cup for him to drink. He did, deeply. Holding the chalice with both hands, he tilted back his head and drained it according to the custom.

He set the empty vessel down. Leaning into Alys he whispered, "Soon I will have nectar of a finer sort to sate me."

Pretending anger, she swatted at his arm. "You shouldna say such wicked things to me on our wedding day and Christmas nay less."

He grinned. "My sweet Alys, in a few short hours, I mean for us to be verra wicked indeed."

They took their seats, the signal for their guests to do the same. Servants bearing ewers of scented water circulated so that the revelers might refresh themselves by washing their hands. A few seats away, Milread settled Alasdair beside her, his bum propped upon pillows, his wee hand wrapped about her crooked fingers. On Callum's left, Father Fearghas stood and offered a prayer of thanksgiving. Afterward, he sat himself again, attacking the platter of pheasant as though this holy day meal might be his last.

With each toast drunk, the guests grew merrier. On Twelfth Night, the most raucous of the feast days, a great king cake would be served. Whomever was served the slice in which the bean was buried would be crowned Lord of Misrule for the remaining celebration, imbued with all manner of privileges including the right to choose his queen. Glancing over at Callum, engaged in conversation with Father Fearghas, Alys had a strong suspicion of who that lucky lord and lady would be.

Atop the table, Callum's hand closed over hers. Beneath it, his other hand found her knee. "Happy?" His expression told her he well knew her answer and yet she gave it anyway.

Beneath the table, she ran her hand along the inside of his thigh. They might not yet be bedded, but so far as she was concerned, the "bold and buxom" part of their celebrating couldn't begin soon enough.

"Happier than I have ever before been or thought to be."

Her hand engulfed in her husband's big, broad palm, she sought to stretch her mind about the breadth of her bounty. From their head table to the trestle tables situated far in the back, the mood was uniformly jovial, the guests' faces wreathed in smiles. How foolish she'd been to think an old wives' tale or a bag of carved stones could threaten their happiness.

She turned back to her bridegroom and smiled. "Pray tell me I'm not dreaming."

He speared a bite-sized bit of capon and fed her from his knife. "You're not dreaming."

Still uneasy with being so catered to, she hesitated and then took the meat into her mouth. Swallowing, she said, "We are truly wed, are we not?"

His low groan funneled into her ear. Beneath the table, his hand carried hers upward to cup his hardness. "By the saints I hope so, for I'm sore sick of this cock-stand I've suffered for seven months. As it is, I find myself hard-pressed not to take you atop one of these fine tables or better yet, forgo the feasting altogether and bear you up to my bed."

Heedless of who might be watching, she tossed back

her head and laughed. She couldn't help it. That was the
magic of Callum. He always knew how to set her at ease.

"After seven months, surely another few hours willna
matter overmuch. It would be churlish to desert our
guests on the First Day of Christmas." She gave his
genitals a slight stroke.

Callum answered with a growl. "Once they fill their
bellies with my beef and make their heads muzzy with
my whiskey and wine, they'll scarce mark whether we
bide here or…above."

"They'll want to bed us proper will they not?" She'd
been so caught up in worrying about the nuptial ceremony that, until now, she hadn't given much thought to
the other wedding rites that might follow.

According to custom, the bride and groom were to
be escorted to their chamber and put to bed before their
guests. Oftentimes the priest led the procession, laying
a blessing upon the couple's heads, but for the most part,
ribald jests and salacious groping ruled the day. A
bride's garter was accounted to be a special prize. A
bachelor who succeeded in snatching it and gifting it to
his lady was said to be guaranteed faithfulness in his
own marriage. But mostly it was all for fun.

His expression darkened. "They may wish to but
they willna, not if I and my dirk have anything to say
of it. Once I have you within those four chamber walls,
the only eyes to feast upon you will be mine and if any
man dares reach for your garter, I'll see his hand cut off
with my own blade. That goes for you, too, Father." He
elbowed Father Fearghas in the side.

The priest laughed. He reached for his wine cup and

washed down the mouthful of capon he'd just polished off. "I've wedded you to this lady proper, my lord. So far as I see it, my duty is done."

Alys looked to where Milread rocked Alasdair upon her lap, sugar glazing his mouth. So far as her son knew, Callum was his father. Someday when he was older she would tell him the sad story of his sire but for the next few years at least she meant for him to enjoy an uncomplicated youth. It hadn't taken either of them long to get used to feeling warm and safe, cherished and loved. There was no point in snatching away the coveted treasure anytime soon.

Throughout the day, guests approached their table, some simply to wish them well, others bearing gifts. Evening shadows fell. The torches were lit. Alys felt her heart skip. Soon she and Callum would kiss over the stack of bride cakes and bid their company good-night. Unlike a virgin bride, she would have no difficulty in keeping her wifely vow. She would know exactly how to rouse and please her lord, to sate his passion whilst stoking it 'til dawn's light. She would employ every whore's trick she knew to bring him pleasure such as he'd never before known and this time she wouldn't feel the slightest shame, for she would be doing so in the service of love.

The parade of approaching guests finally abated. Most were likely too drunk to stand. Alys's pulse quickened. She gave a quick glance to the arched doorway. It led to the turret stairs, which in turn led to Callum's solar and their bridal bower. Soon, very soon, she and her lord would take leave of their guests and retire to that longed-for private place. After seven long months, clothes would be shed and passions unleashed. Alys licked her lips. Mayhap it was the oyster she'd earlier eaten, but she could almost taste the brine of her beloved's skin.

A tinker rose from one of the lower tables, a great pack slung over his broad shoulder and his cloak hood drawn high over his head. Seeing him start toward them, Alys silently cursed. As touched as she was by the displays of fealty, she so wanted to be alone with her lord. Beyond that, he was either odd or unpardonably rude. Every other man from the most humble crofter to the mightiest warrior had shown his respect by baring his head upon entering. And the man's gait was all wrong. Most tradesmen adopted a mincing step and slope-shouldered stance when approaching the nobility. Not so this man. Long, confident strides bore him up the aisle between trestles to the front of the hall, his heavy warrior's boots striking the slates and scattering the fresh rushes laid down that morn.

Reaching them, he stopped at the dais steps and bowed deeply. "My lord, my lady." His English-accented voice sounded scratchy yet strangely familiar.

Callum spoke up. "You are either verra brave or verra stupid to come here, Outlander."

The tinker didn't deny it. "I come in peace and with your permission would offer my humble gift to the beautiful bride."

Callum nodded. "It is my wedding day and Christmas, both fine reasons for setting aside fealties and feuding."

The tradesman inclined his covered head. "I thank

you." He opened his cloak and spread the sides wide, displaying pockets lined with all manner of wares. "I have any number of fineries befitting a lady's fancy: pearls to complement her creamy skin, rings and earbobs set with sapphires to bring out the celestial blue of her eyes, silk ribbons to festoon her sun-kissed tresses."

Callum bent his face to Alys, his warm breath striking her ear. "The jewels are paste to be sure but you might as well choose one so as not to give offense. The sooner he leaves, the sooner we can retire."

She stared down into the foreigner's hooded face, and the foreboding she'd earlier dismissed struck her in the stomach with full force. Mayhap it was his hood which brought to mind images of the Grim Reaper, but the thought of taking anything of his repulsed her.

She shook her head. "Good tinker, I thank you but there is nay thing I need or want. By the dust on your boots, you must have brought your bundle a great way. I would leave you to peddle your wares to the castle folk."

It was no more than the truth. Considering all the rich gifts she'd received already, she couldn't fathom wanting or needing a single thing. What she dearly wanted was for the man to be on his way so that she and Callum might retire upstairs.

He stood in place, fixing her with his hidden gaze. Peering more closely, she understood why he wished to keep his face in shadow. Though she could make out little beyond the cleft splitting his squared chin, she saw that the flesh was shiny with scars.

"Come, my lady, everyone desires…something. I have in my bag some very fine bolts of silks and satins, as well. Mayhap you might fancy one of them for a gown, something in yellow, I think?"

Yellow! Alys felt the room begin to reel. Why did it always come back to yellow? She'd thought herself done with that corrupted color but it seemed she was not. Tinkers traveled great distances. Might he have seen her plying the prostitute's trade in Portree? Had he come to expose her? That fearful thought led to one viler yet. What if she'd serviced him! If so, not even Callum could redeem her. Even a laird must answer to his council, his people. Would his trusted advisors, the "old gentlemen," stand aside and allow their laird to take a former whore as his consort?

Beside her Callum stiffened. His broad shoulder brushed her. Out of the corner of her eye, she saw the vein in the center of his forehead commence pulsing, a telltale sign he was very angry indeed.

"You heard my lady. She does not care for your gifts nor do I care for your insolent manner. Take up your pack and get you gone from my hall—*now*." Beneath the table, his big hand covered hers.

"And so I will but first I would bear away with me that, or rather those you have taken from me."

Callum let go of Alys's hand and leapt to his feet. Bracing his palms on the table, he leaned over like a lion poised to pounce. "There is nay thing here that belongs to you, churl. Be gone!"

But the tinker lifted his scarred chin, squared his shoulders, and held his ground. "Would the laird of the Frasers willfully steal another man's property, even if that man was English? I come in peace. But whether in peace or war, I will have my property returned to me."

Callum reached down and drew his dirk from its sheath. "Let us see your face, knave. I would look a man in the eye before I send him to his maker."

"As you wish." The tinker reached up and swept back his hood.

Even through the mask of scars, Alys knew him.

A phantom's face.

An English face.

Her husband, Alex's face.

A black curtain fell about her, heavy and fast. Her soft-soled slippers seemed to melt into the floor, the rest of her limbs going boneless and weak. The shocked faces and high-pitched murmurings, and finally, the very light—all were veiled from her. Weightless as a cloud, she swayed. She spun. She spiraled. She fell back, grateful to the blissful blackness bearing her far, far away.

TURNING TO LOOK out onto the company, the Outlander lifted his arms and called out, "I am Alexander Field and this lady is prior wed—to me!"

Heads swung to the front of the room. Eyes popped and mouths hung open. Above them, the musicians ceased playing. Instead of sweet music, whispered exclamations of "Sassenach," "Outlander," and "liar" filled the chamber.

Pitching his voice above them, Field went on, "We were wed in St. Andrew's of Portree nigh on two years ago. The parish records will bear me out."

Callum drew out his dirk and roared, "Silence, knave!" He might have lunged over the table and dispatched the Outlander then and there but a swift glance back at Alys showed his lady to have swooned in her seat.

Holding her upright against him, he motioned for Milread. Moving with a swiftness that belied her years and blindness, the wise woman rose from her chair and appeared at his side.

Frantic, he grabbed the urn, doused his hand, and slapped water onto Alys's parchment-pale cheeks. Looking to Milread, he demanded, "Rouse her. Rouse her now. She must deny him. She must!"

Sad-faced, the wise woman shook her head. For the first time since Callum had known her, she neither cackled nor grinned. "Were I to awaken her, I dinna believe she could do as you ask."

Callum whirled on Field. The Outlander grinned, a brilliant white smile splitting his fouled face, the image bringing to mind the gargoyles snarling down from the parapets of cathedrals. "Faith, I always could make her swoon."

Callum knew the fiend goaded him and yet he was hard-pressed not to plunge his dirk into that ravaged throat.

He handed Alys off to Father Fearghas with instructions to carry her to her chamber. He and the priest had had their differences in the past and yet his former tutor was the only man beyond his brother whom he would entrust with his lady's care.

He waited until she was borne away before turning

back to Field. Patchy blond hair framed a face that was at once pathetic and grotesque. Faces ravaged by smallpox were common sights, the lifelong pitting a badge of survivorship, but Callum had never before seen a disfigurement so severe. Like a riverbed flooded and then drained dry, rivulets of shiny scarlet scars slashed across his flesh from forehead to chin. The gullies ran deepest on the right side of his face, puckering his full mouth and lifting one side in what looked to be a permanent sneer. Under other circumstances, he would have found himself moved to pity.

But Callum had no pity to spare for this man, none at all. Had he his bow with him, Field might already be dead. Watching his bride being borne away, he allowed that the Outlander might yet not survive the night.

Spearing the dirk in the air, he said, "You must know you court death by proclaiming such."

Field shrugged his shoulders, nearly as broad as Callum's. "I have courted death before, Scotsman, and cheated her, as well. The smallpox may have stripped the flesh from my bones but by God I willna let it strip my family from me, as well. I claim what is mine by right, my wife and my son." His gaze darted to Alasdair, happily banging his spoon on the tabletop.

Callum felt fresh fury wash over him. The Outlander was broadly and blatantly playing to the crowd. Judging from the looks on their faces, he'd already won considerable sympathy. When it came to manipulating human emotions, apparently ugliness could be as useful as fairness. He stabbed his dirk into the table, splitting the board.

Glaring at Field over the quivering hilt, he said, "Until I can unravel this coil, you, Englishman, will remain here."

"You would toss me in your dungeon, then, so that you may make my wife your whore?" Again that aggrieved tone and carrying voice proclaiming himself as both the hero and the victim.

Callum had never before faced such a fight. They stood in his great hall, Alys was his wife, and yet the Outlander had maneuvered events so that he was the one on the defensive.

And so Callum retaliated the only way he knew, with threats he would not hesitate to prove. "Dinna try me, knave. I am laird here, and you are far removed from the protection of your English king. I can do with you as I will. I *shall* do with you as I will. Make no mistake, Outlander. Whilst you remain within these castle walls, you are subject to one man's will and one man's only—mine."

THEY SAT on opposing sides of the trestle table in Callum's solar, taking one another's measure. Callum was the first to speak. "What is it you want?"

Field plucked an apple from the bowl between them. So far in private he'd shown himself to be soft-spoken, almost relaxed.

He bit into the fruit. Callum saw that his teeth were white and strong and perfect, yet another contrast. "I would have thought I'd made myself plain. I want my wife and my son back with me in London where they belong."

Callum couldn't hold back. "London!" Ere now he'd been so caught up in combating Field's claim he hadn't considered that the man might mean to take Alys and Alasdair so very far away. But of course England was his home. Once they crossed the border, his lady and her son would be beyond Callum's protection. "I will not allow it."

Field shook his head. "You cannot stop it. Alys is my wife and the boy, my son."

"I could make you disappear?"

Field bit into the apple again, sending juice spurting. Chewing, he said, "I've just ruined your wedding feast and claimed your bride. Were I to go missing, you'd be a murderer in the eyes of every man and woman in your clan. From what little I know of tanistry, lairds lead by the will of their people, not strictly speaking, by birthright. Would your fellow Frasers consent to be led by a chief who was a cold-blooded murderer and a bigamist in the bargain? I think not."

Watching him, Callum allowed he'd never wanted anyone dead more. "I could have you tortured. A few turns on the rack would have you singing a different song."

He was bluffing or at least he started out that way. His dungeon was a series of holding cells. To his knowledge, he didn't possess so much as a thumb screw. But if the threat of torture or even torture itself caused Alexander Field to renounce his claim on Alys, by God he'd have a fleet of racks carted in.

The knave seemed more amused than cowed. "Whatever you've in mind, I hope it won't spoil my looks."

"What is it you want? Money, then? Land? Cattle? It can't be easy earning your bread now." Callum would gladly relinquish all his earthly wealth if it meant keeping Alys and her son with him.

Field paused in palming the fruit. The snarl on his face suggested Callum had found a weak spot.

"The smallpox may have made my face ugly as sin, but I can wield a sword as ably as ever I could."

"Prove it." Pressing his advantage, Callum surged to his feet. He reached for his dirk. "An English broad sword against a Scottish claymore, what say you?"

From the doorway, Alys cried out, "Callum, nay!"

If anyone could render him weak, it was his lady. Callum couldn't trust himself to look at her. He needed to stay strong and from the first day he'd set eyes upon her, he'd been nothing but weak where she was concerned. "Alys, leave me to handle this."

Field rose, as well. He tossed the apple core into the rushes and turned toward her. "Sweetheart, I've come for you at last." He opened his arms.

She hesitated, looking from one man to the other. After a moment, she rushed to Callum's side, laying a staying hand upon his arm. "You cannot challenge him. I will not be the cause of spilled blood."

Aware of Field watching, Callum took her into his arms and smoothed a soothing hand along her spine. *I don't care what his game is. You're mine. Mine!*

"Dinna fret, dearling. This is a matter to be settled among men."

"There is nothing to settle." She pulled back and turned her face up to his, her blue eyes beseeching. "He speaks true. I am his wife. Alasdair is his son. He has every right to claim us."

Callum hadn't expected that. Ere now he'd convinced himself the tinker, Field, must be a skilled actor, a fraud. "Alys, nay!"

She looked over his shoulder to Field. "I will go with you on the morrow."

He nodded. "Of course you will. You are a good and dutiful wife." He caught Callum's gaze and added, "*My* wife."

Callum felt the muscle ticking in his jaw. It was the same sensation he'd had just before he'd taken deadly aim and shot his arrow into Brianna's treacherous advisor, Duncan. That act had been in the service of saving three lives, his brother's, Brianna's and Alys's. Killing Alexander Field would be pure pleasure.

Callum released Alys and put her behind him. He pulled his dirk from its sheath and advanced on Field. Field, too, unsheathed the sword from his side. The Outlander was a goodly sized man but Callum was the taller and broader-shouldered of them.

Closing in on his enemy, Callum relished how Field had to look up to him. "Let us settle this once and for all, Outlander." Dirk in hand, he lunged.

Alys darted forward. "My lord, nay!" She threw herself between them, blocking his thrust.

Callum drew back. Muscles trembling, he forced his weapon arm back down to his side. Thinking how close he'd come to cutting Alys, sweat broke out upon his brow. Such loss of control in a trained warrior was all but unforgivable. He'd attacked many times before, killed even, but never in the heat of the moment. The blood lust upon him was more potent than whiskey—and far more deadly.

He caught a sideways look at Alys's frightened face and sheathed his knife. "I should kill you and be done with the deed," he said to Field.

Alexander shrugged. "Murder is murder even if I am English. You'd not only lose the support of your clansmen but also place Alys in direst peril."

Callum scraped a hand through his sweat-dampened hair. "Alys, how so?" The murderous rage was abating, leaving him muzzy-headed and physically weak.

Gentling his voice, Field answered, "The penalty for adultery is stoning. That is so not only in England but in Scotland, as well, I think."

His gaze shifted to Alys, standing with her back flattened against the wall. Callum didn't miss how those light-lashed eyes followed the line and curve of her body. Even pale and frightened, she was so incredibly, irresistibly beautiful.

The Outlander's gaze wended its way back to him. "I saw the body of a stoning victim once, a whore who'd run afoul of the parish priest. Her face and form were all but unrecognizable for all she'd been a beauty in life." Dividing his gaze between them, he pulled what passed for a pitying face. "I shall retire to my—our—chamber and leave you in privacy to say your goodbyes."

THE DOOR FELL CLOSED behind Alexander. Left alone, Alys turned to Callum across what was to have been their bridal bower. Upon the trestle table a simple matrimonial supper had been laid out for later—dates and figs, walnuts and pistachios, sundry cheeses, a bowl of fruit, and a flagon of wine to quench their thirst and abet conception—all the ingredients of a joyous and fruitful first night together.

Callum came toward her. "Deny him, Alys. Deny him for the madman he must be to come here. One word from you, and I will have him escorted to the English border in irons. Deny him and all will yet be well, as it was before between us, as if he never set foot here."

She shook her head, which felt weighted as with lead. "I canna, for he speaks true. He is Alexander Field, my husband. Much changed though he is, still I know him. Beyond any doubt, he is my lawful husband."

He drew back his arm and crashed his fist upon the table, causing the bowls to jump. "I dinna care who he is, deny him. You can. You must! For both our sakes, you must. It is the only way."

Alys swallowed hard. How she wished she might faint again and thereby have some reprieve from the pain. "He has made his claim public before your clansmen. Even were he to rescind it and go away, the damage is done. Your counselors, the Old Gentlemen, would never countenance a bigamous marriage. And not even a laird can command a priest to shrive so blasphemous an act. It is too late, my lord. We love but too late."

For the first time since they'd met, he touched her with less than gentleness. He seized her by the shoulders and dealt her a shake, the force knocking her veil askew. "It is not too late. I willna let it be too late."

His fingers dug into her forearms and Alys welcomed the pain. How she hoped there would be bruising on the morrow, something of him to take away with her for a little while at least.

"You must let me go, my lord. You must let me go to my husband."

Blue eyes slammed into hers, a battering ram to her heart. "You would go to his bed, then? You would render such honor to the man who deserted you? Who left you to starve and then stayed away for these two years. Mind I ken your history, lady. Were it not for the burgher's widow stealing Alasdair away, and you coming to the MacLeod's court to plead your case before Brianna, you would still be lifting your skirts to secure your son's bread."

Never before had he spoken to her so harshly but then, never before had he had such abundant cause. "He didn't know of my troubles. You've only to look at his scars to see how sick he has been."

Callum released her, staring as though she'd grown a second head. "Do you defend him, then?"

"Nay, I mean, aye." At her wit's end, she threw her hands up in the air. "He is my husband and the father of my son. What choice have I?"

"You could choose to stay with me."

It was Alys's turn to anger. How simple he made it all seem. "And make myself not only a whore again but also an adulteress? Damn the immortal soul of the man I love to Hellfire through my selfishness and lust? Lose my son?"

"You will not lose your son. I will not allow it."

"Will you not? Look me in the eye, my lord, and swear to me upon our love that you can stop Alex from taking away my son."

He couldn't and they both knew it. The fierce determination that had marked his features descended to defeat. He scraped a hand through his hair, pushing back that rebellious raven forelock she so loved. "Promise you'll come to me tomorrow morn before you set out."

To speak of farewells on what was to have been their wedding night! Close to crying, she shook her head. "My lord—"

His gaze locked on hers. "Promise me. This canna be our goodbye, it canna."

She glimpsed the sheen in his eyes and knew he was holding back tears, too. Her proud, bold Callum was on the verge of weeping—for her, for them, for the future of beautiful, everlasting Christmases that now would never be.

Overcome, she nodded. "Verra well, I will come."

Callum ran his hands along her upper arms, raising gooseflesh. Bringing his face close to hers, he held her gaze and whispered, "Stay with me tonight."

"I canna, you know I canna."

His warm breath brushed her lips. "Stay with me. If we must part on the morrow, then let us do so as lovers."

She shook her head, tears welling. "To lie together would damn both our souls."

"Stay with me," he begged, his evergreen scent flooding her senses and clouding her mind. "Stay with me and let us burn together, for I'd writhe in Satan's flames with you before I'd occupy Paradise with any other." His hand found her nape, his thumb stroking a suddenly sensitive spot. "Stay with me."

Liquid warmth rushed between her legs, her body lustfully alive for all that her heart was breaking. Callum must have sensed she was on the verge of surrender.

Cradling her head, he deepened the kiss, running his tongue along the seam of her lips, urging her to open. "Kisses, only kisses…"

This time he was lying, and they both knew it. If she stayed with him, they would share a great deal more than kisses. She was no widow now, but a married woman. If they made love, she would be damning not only her immortal soul but Callum's, as well. As much as she wanted him, she loved him even more. Reaching for what willpower she had left, she planted both palms against his chest and pushed. He was solid, implacable as a mountain. She couldn't begin to move him and yet he fell back of his own accord, expression shocked and so very wounded.

Seeing the hurt in his eyes, knowing she'd put it there, proved to be her undoing. "Oh, Callum…" Before she might yet do more harm, she turned and ran from the room.

4

AFTER LEAVING Alys with Callum, Alex had sought out a servant who'd grudgingly pointed him the way to her chamber. He walked about the room, examining the sundry finery, touching all her fragile, pretty things. Stroking a finger over the ivory-backed brush, he caught his reflection in the mirror and stared. By now he should be used to the face staring back at him but he wasn't. That visage still seemed to belong to a fair-day freak, a stranger.

After leaving a very pregnant Alys in Portree nearly two years ago, he'd struck out for England. He'd been in London less than a sennight when the smallpox symptoms struck. For five days he lay racked with fever, pains searing his head, back and body's muscles. On the fifth day the sweating started and the blistering broke out. It was almost a relief. Black blood bubbled beneath the surface pustules. He might have been mistaken for a burning victim who'd survived the stake but barely. He hadn't really expected to live. Once he realized he would, he was vain enough not to want those who'd known him before to see his disfigurement. He'd had the letter sent to Alys. He reasoned it wasn't entirely a lie. The handsome man with whom she'd eloped and come north was dead indeed. As for her, a blind man could have marked her beauty. Pregnant or not, she'd have no difficulty finding another protector.

He turned away from his reflection, seeking happier vistas. Taking in the well-appointed room, the windows paned with glass, not shuttered, the bed-hangings brocaded and richly embroidered, he admitted Alys had done better for herself than he had ever imagined. Some Highland lairds might still live among their cattle and sheep but not this one. Callum Fraser was a wealthy man. Earlier he'd observed that the great hall was paneled and freshly painted, the walls bedecked with costly tapestries, the carved wooden chairs and benches suggesting Italian artistry. The strap-work screen concealing the minstrel's gallery alone must have cost a small fortune. Even for a holy day and a wedding, the fare was exceptionally fine. The bread served at even the lowest table where he'd earlier sat was finely milled grain.

The chamber door opened, interrupting his thoughts. Alys entered, the child in her arms.

"I thought you would want to meet your son." She came toward him. "I named him Alasdair after you."

He stared down at the boy. Blond-haired, blue-eyed and pink-cheeked, his son was bonny as a babe could be. "He's healthy?"

Maternal pride shone from her cornflower-blue eyes. "Praise be to God he is. As you can see, he's a good eater."

Even before the sickness, he'd never been good with children. Feeling like a fish out of water, he leaned closer. "Well, now, you're a fine lad, aren't you?" He stretched out a finger to test the creamy smoothness of that baby cheek, thinking that was how his skin had used to be.

Alasdair lifted his head from his mother's shoulder. He looked back at Alex. His blue eyes, the same shape as his mother's, grew black and big. He rolled back his lips and screamed.

Alex reared back, his right eye twitching. He'd thought himself inured to children's taunts and terror but he'd been wrong. The rejection from his own flesh-and-blood burned like a pox blister.

"Take him away! Take him from my sight."

Alys rubbed her hand along their son's shuddering shoulders. Atop the din, she said, "He's just a baby. He needs time. He'll become accustomed—"

"I said take him away!"

The sickness had left his hearing overly sensitive. The babe's bawling felt like needles piercing his ears. He covered them with his hands, the screaming carrying him back to that terrible time when the death cart came 'round, the black and blistered bodies heaped like cordwood, the lifeless limbs dangling off the side.

Atop the tolling bell, the cart driver's call rang out, "Bring out your dead. Bring out your dying…"

And from behind every shuttered window and X-marked door came a cacophony of terrible, ceaseless weeping.

MILREAD WRAPPED HERSELF in her cloak, took up her staff, and ventured out into the night. She passed through the portcullis without incident, gained the gate-house, and padded down the packed-earth path toward the copse. Standing on its edge, she turned to look back at the castle. Built several centuries ago, the fortress was of standard design, two circular towers flanking a central keep. A lone figure stood on the crenellated parapet wall, aggrieved gaze staring out onto the black vastness, blind to all save his loss and pain.

Callum Fraser.

Milread clutched at her heart, which suddenly felt bruised to the point of bleeding. Even from a distance, she could feel his suffering seeping inside her like a great gray fog, penetrating her tissue and bone.

Cursing Alexander Field, she saved some curses back for herself, as well. Her lady, Brianna had charged her with Alys's care. She should have better protected her wean. Instead of spending Christmastide Eve scattering rose petals and bullying bridegrooms, she ought to have employed all her arts to come up with a talisman to lessen the rune cast's portent of ill fortune. Runes had uses beyond divination. One who'd studied the ancient symbols as she had could use them to make magick both black and white. Alys's husband's deformity would draw pity from many, those who used only their two physical eyes for seeing, but beyond his fouled flesh his aura was putrid green and pitted with great gaping black holes. Tempted as she was to hurl a hex at him that would make the smallpox seem mild, she held back. Fate would take care of the Outlander in its own good time. Her present concern was Alys and the Fraser. To Freya, the Norse goddess of love, she offered up a silent prayer that it might not be too late.

She continued on her way, keeping her Third Eye open and her ears pricked for the guiding whispers of the gods. Bypassing fallen trees and moss-covered branches, she continued her search. For her purpose, dead wood would never do. When she came to the spot, she stopped. The tree wasn't the tallest or grandest or oldest by any means, and yet she knew with complete surety it was the one. The slender yew was scarcely more than a sapling and yet, like the Lady Alys, it showed great promise for future growth. The yew was also the Fraser clan badge, its symbol of protection.

Concentrating on her purpose, she circled the tree nine times. When she'd completed the final circuit, she stopped, bowed and asked for its branch and blessing.

"Hail to thee, O tree of yew!

I crave the boon of your branch.

So that it may aid me in my healing work,

To mend that wound which otherwise would sever two lovers' hearts."

Satisfied, she withdrew the small saw from her bag and hacked off one of the low-lying branches. Again, with the tree's permission, she split it into nine like-sized pieces. Filling the sack she'd brought, she dragged her burden back to the castle and up the spiraling stairs, praying to the gods for strength and willing herself not to feel the weight.

Back in her chamber, she lit a fire, pulled her chair up to it, and laid the nine pieces of severed limb upon her lap. She took out her short knife. For hours, she sat rocking and humming and whittling until she had nine rounded runes. By dawn's break she held each piece up and made the vertical slashes for the sacred symbols upon which she'd meditated all the night.

As she had the night before, she spread the white cloth, only instead of casting she laid out the nine runes in a neatly scripted line. She began with EIHWAZ and EOLH, both runes of protection, and much needed in the current case, for she didn't trust Alexander Field any farther than she might throw him.

KENAZ followed, bringing male strength, energy and power; this rune represented Callum.

Next LAGAZ, the rune of female power and intuition, represented Alys.

MANNAZ so that aid might arrive in good time and in whatever form needed.

ING represented deliverance from the problem at hand.

TIR AND SIGEL, both runes of victory, she set side by side.

She ended with WUNJO for a happy outcome, lasting joy.

Running her hands above the runes without touching them, feeling their energy flow through her, Milread bowed her heavy head and prayed.

"O mighty Odin, King of the Gods,

And Frigga, Mother of all that is good and holy,

I pray you guide and protect the lass known as Alys and the lord known as Callum Fraser.

Grant them your wisdom and the courage and might of Thor.

By the powers of Earth, Wind, Fire and Water, so mote it be!"

IT WAS TO HAVE BEEN her wedding night.

Wrapped in Callum's silk-lined tartan, Alys stood at the bedchamber window, tracing senseless shapes on the frosted pane with a single cold-numbed finger. She'd undressed for bed a while ago, and still she couldn't bring herself to go near it—or her husband.

In the midst of her misery, the irony of the situation wasn't lost on her. Every day for the months after Alex had left her in Portree, she'd prayed to Saint Michael, the patron saint of soldiers, to bring him safely back to her. Even after the priest read the letter proclaiming him dead, a part of her had held on to the hope that there must be some mistake, that he lived still. Now all her heartfelt prayers had been answered, and what she wouldn't give to see every one of them undone.

As much as it pained her to think of leaving Scotland, Alex's taking them to his homeland, to England, would likely prove to be a good thing. The nearness with which she'd come to surrendering to Callum's plea to stay with him and damning both their souls by the willful commission of adultery terrified her. It would be far better for the both of them to make their break a clean one than to languish in proximity, physically close and yet hopelessly apart. In time his heart would heal. He would move forward with his life, marry and make a family. The thought of him holding another woman wrenched her, but above all she wanted him to be happy. She wanted him to be whole.

"Come to bed, Alys," Alex called to her. Propped upon the pillows and sipping his second cup of Callum's wine, he regarded her with an inscrutable gaze.

"I will come anon. I'm not yet sleepy."

"Neither am I." His ironic tone wasn't lost on her.

She turned away from the window, cursing herself for an insensitive sot. "Oh, Alex, I'm—"

"Sorry, I know. Pray don't be. I know I'm much changed, and yet I'm still the same man you wed, the same man you said you loved."

"Are you?"

His earlier outburst had unnerved her. For the first time since she'd put Alasdair to bed and returned to the room, she let herself look at him, truly look at him. It wasn't only his face that was changed. There was a hardness to his eyes she didn't remember from before. He might have been a stranger.

"Where have you been all this time, Alex? I know you were ill," she added, anticipating his excuse, "but two years... All this time you've let me think you dead. Why?"

He yanked back the coverlet, swung his legs over the bedside and rose. "I was dead or the nearest thing to it." He crossed the chamber toward her. His footfalls kept perfect pace with her pounding heart. "The physician didn't expect me to live. I didn't expect me to live. When I dictated that letter, I believed myself to be but hours from death. I wanted to write you whilst I was still in my right mind."

Unexpected rage welled up inside her. "You had it written as if you were dead already!"

"My only aim was to spare you, Alys. Whatever wrong I committed was done for love of you. You must believe me."

She bowed her head. Really what did it matter now? "I want to believe you."

He reached her. She steeled herself to neither flinch nor look away. "And after?"

"I was so ill and weak, I couldn't be certain I'd live to rise from those stinking, fouled sheets. Once I did…" He spread his arms out from his sides. His twisted lip trembled. "The first thing I asked for, demanded, was a mirror. When I saw myself or rather what was left of me, I didn't see how you could still want me. You're so beautiful, Alys." Eyes damp, he reached out and stroked a finger down the side of her face.

Suffering his touch, she swallowed hard, guilt warring with what was likely a very unfair anger. Had he sent for her, the scars wouldn't have mattered. She would have found a way to go to him, to be with him. But he hadn't sent for her. And because of that she'd become a whore. He was right. Now she didn't want him, not because of his scars but because she wanted, *loved*, another. She loved Callum of the raven hair and wicked blue eyes and steadfast heart. Callum who was always there for her no matter how unsuitable she might be. Callum who might have had his choice of any highborn Scots ladies and yet still had chosen her to be his bride.

Callum who just that morning she'd pledged to love with the whole of her mind and body and heart for the rest of her days. And yet two years before she'd made a similar pledge to this man, to Alex. Was she truly so fickle?

"Two years is a long time to live without hope." The stony timbre of her voice surprised her. She scarcely recognized herself. How cold she sounded, how flat.

He dropped his arm to his side. "He is handsome, your Scotsman."

Contrite, she reached for him. "Alex, it's not about—"

His pale, plaintive gaze fell on her face. "We can snuff the candles, keep the chamber dark. Mayhap in the dark, you won't mind as much. We'll make a game of it. You used to fancy games." In the flickering light, his eyes glowed.

She shook her head, feeling weary and old for all that she was not yet twenty. "Alex, I'm not a child."

"Close your eyes and pretend I am as I once was. Pretend we are as we once were, young and gay and making a bed of the sweet-smelling straw in your parents' barn, you begging me to cease tickling you for fear that your giggling would wake them."

It wasn't only Alex who'd changed. When they'd met, she'd been so very young and unschooled in the ways of men, her safe little life revolving around her Da's dairy and market days in their village. And then one day the cow she was minding broke free. Knowing its worth, she'd run after the animal blindly. Without realizing it, she'd crossed into Outlander territory and run smack into an English foot patrol. In his domed helmet and chain mail and carrying a spear as tall as she, the soldier approaching her was a fearsome sight. But when he drew up before her, she saw that he was also winsome and young and smiling. He handed her back the roped cow, his warning softened by a kiss. Alys had never before been kissed on other than her cheek. Fuzzy-headed and warm in places she'd never before credited, she opened her eyes and looked up at him. His face was fair, his smile beguiling, his words honeyed. They started meeting in secret, he wooing her with head-turning compliments and grand tales of the adventures he'd had in his English lord's service. It wasn't long before the talking ceased and the touching commenced. And Alasdair was conceived.

She hugged the plaid closer, pretending the comforting cloth was Callum's arms. "We can't go back."

She hadn't meant to raise her voice but doing so made the pronouncement no less true. They couldn't go back. Even if they could, she no longer wanted to.

"We can. We will!" She couldn't be sure but she thought he might have stamped his foot. The Alex she'd known and aye, loved, would never show such petulance. "Don't you want to, Alys? Don't you want me?"

In truth, she didn't. But though she loved Callum, she owed Alex her absolute loyalty. It was a terrible conundrum. Feeling as if she was a wishbone being pulled in twain, she shook her head in helplessness. "I pray you be patient with me. I need…time."

He exhaled heavily and nodded. "Very well, I will not force myself on you, not this night nor during our journey." His eyes hardened. "But once we are in London, I will expect you to be a wife to me in every way."

"Of course." She hugged Callum's plaid about her, drawing bittersweet comfort from its clinging evergreen scent. "Thank you."

His terms were more than fair, generous even. As his wife, her body belonged to him. He was within his rights to claim her whenever he would and yet he was willingly granting her time to become accustomed to him.

Wanting to be fair in return, she said, "Once we are in England, whatever means of employ you choose to pursue, I will work hard to be a help to you." She forced herself to reach across and take his hand. Beyond a crater or two, it was unblemished.

It would be hard for her, a Scot, to blend in, let alone belong, but she would do her very best to find her place, for her son's sake as well as Alex's. Growing up in the Borders, Alex wasn't the only Outlander—English person—she'd encountered. She could mimic a passable English accent when she was called upon to do so. What had started out as a game to amuse her younger siblings had developed into a talent she would need to call upon for the very near future.

And she would. Loving Callum was a fixed, unalterable state. She could no more change it than she could change the color of her eyes from blue to brown or her hair from pale gold to raven's black. But for Alasdair's sake, she was resolved to make this marriage work.

He nodded. Beneath the scars, his taut features seemed to slacken. "What you lack in breeding, you more than make up for in beauty."

Even though he'd been gone from her life for years now, the backhanded compliment stung. Despite her low station, Callum had always shown her the utmost courtesy and respect. Her almost lord always had seemed so very proud to be with her. She hadn't yet left his castle walls and already her heart ached with missing him.

They ended the night by climbing into opposite sides of the bed. Alex drew the curtains closed around them and then fell asleep almost immediately. Lying awake beside him, Alys considered that mayhap the aftermath of the sickness had left him weak. Still it seemed strange to her that their reunion should have so little effect upon him. Her back turned to him, she spent hours listening to his snoring. Did Callum snore, she wondered? She would so dearly love to know. She'd lost her chance to discover that along with so many other precious domestic details.

Sometime before dawn Alex awoke, the rope bed dipping slightly as he rose. Alys had yet to close her eyes. She squeezed them shut then, feigning sleep. The sounds of water splashing and rustling about the chamber told her he must be rising for the day. Taking no chances, she kept her head rooted to the pillow. She lay on her side, her back to him. A while later his footfalls faded, the door creaked open and then closed, signaling his departure.

She sat up with a sigh. The fire had long ago died, leaving the chamber icy as a tomb. Ordinarily she would burrow back beneath the covers and try going back to sleep. But the bed was now a tainted place. Rather than remain there, she rose.

She picked up Callum's plaid, wrapped the chilly wool about her, and settled into the chair by the window to await the dawn. Tucking her legs beneath her, she stared out onto the stillness. It might be Christmas, the season of hope and new beginnings, but inside her soul it felt more like Lent. Her future, which had seemed so bright just yesterday, now loomed before her, unbearably barren, hopelessly bleak, a trial of days and

nights to be endured rather than one of unending Christmases to be celebrated.

Just kisses, only kisses…

She'd tested him for seven long months, needing to
know that his feelings for her were true love, not fickle
fancy. Throughout, he'd proven himself, his love,
many times over. He loved her, he truly loved her. And
now that she was finally and completely certain of his
heart, she must say goodbye to him, not for seven
months or even seven years but for the rest of their
lives. Tears squeezed out of her eyes, slid down her
cheeks. Now she understood why so many women
who'd suffered tragedy and who could afford to do so
retired to convents. A lifetime of no Christmas and no
Callum stretched before her, an unending winter's
night.

She accepted the bleak consequences as her due.
Pregnant or not, marrying Alex had been her choice. But
she could not, would not, condemn Callum to a similar
bleakness. She had pined for Alex for months. Callum,
she feared, would mourn her, their lost love, for the rest
of his days.

The temporal world could be a hard place indeed,
but she knew what she must do to make it that much
easier for Callum. She must release him, not just from
the vows he'd made in church but from the invisible
bonds shackling his heart to hers. Those bonds she
must sever. And so when she took her final leave of him
later that morning, she would also take back her love,
not the feeling but the words. Doing so would all but

kill her. It would mean living the rest of her life as a lie.

But for Callum's future happiness, she would brave the devil himself.

SHE CAME TO HIM that morning as promised. She came to him clad in her blue gown and veiled not as a bride would be but more in the way of a novice nun, the wimple and drape covering the sides of her face as well as her hair. She came to him not with a new wife's bright eyes and glad bearing but with the somber face and measured steps befitting a mourner.

Callum rose from his chair before the banked fire, the same seat from which he'd watched the dawn break. Everything he'd ever loved, everything he'd ever wanted, and everything he now could never have stood on the threshold of his chamber, her one small slipper-shod foot left out in the corridor. Now that Alys was here, he found himself at a loss for words. Unlike his brother, he was a warrior, not a poet, a man more at home with a bow and arrow than a book, a man of action and few words.

He swallowed hard. "You came."

She stepped inside. "As I promised I would."

His gaze scoured her face. The redness rimming her eyes and the faint bluish circles crowning her cheekbones betrayed that she'd wept recently and slept not at all. What he couldn't tell from looking at her was whether or not Field had claimed his husbandly rights. The thought of the Outlander's hands on her had kept him awake all the night.

Crossing toward him, she glanced about the derelict

chamber. He well knew what she was seeing. Rose petals lay brown and curled upon the turned-down bed, the bed in which he still refused to lay himself to rest. On the table what was to have been their wedding supper sat out untouched, the bread and cheese molding, the candlestick still lying on its side. For now he wanted nothing touched.

"I feared you might not." He who'd never feared anything in his misbegotten life, had feared never seeing her again with all his might.

Drawing up before him, she admitted, "I nearly didna. I've always loathed goodbyes. But to steal away without seeing you would be the coward's way, would it not? And I needed to give you…this."

She reached for his hand and without thinking he gave it, so eager was he to touch and be touched by her. Too late he realized her intent. The signet ring lay cold and heavy in his palm. She closed his fingers about it.

Taking back his token was like a knife twisting in his heart. He slammed the ring down on the table. "I don't want it. Keep it."

She shook her head, so firm, so adamant. "It is meant for your bride."

He closed the small space between them and wrapped his arms about her in a fiercely possessive hug. "You are my bride, you and nay other!" He buried his face in the sweet curve of her throat and shoulder, the damnable veil getting in his way.

"My lord, I beg of you…" Her voice broke.

She tried stepping back but he tightened his hold. "I dinna care if he's your lawful husband. Forsake him and bide here with me. Married or not, shriven or not, acknowledged or not, I vow to love you and protect you and keep myself to you and only you for the rest of my days." He bowed his burning forehead against her cool one.

"I know you do, but you mustn't." She took his face between her hands and looked up into his welling eyes. "You are young and strong and beautiful and one day ere long you will find a good lady to love, a bride who is worthy of you and free to love you openly and without shame, who can give you fine, strong sons."

Who could have predicted that in the final leave-taking, she would be the strong one, the comforter? But then his life ere now had been so very easy while hers had been so very painful and hard.

"I willna." He caught her hand and carried it to his lips. "Living without you, lady, is an art I've no wish to learn."

She shook her head. "Learn it you must. You must!" Her voice was firm for all its softness. "You must find the strength to let me go and I you. We must say goodbye now lest we court a greater grief in the future. My lord, if you love me, let me go!"

His hands fell away. He dragged a hand through his hair, deliberately scouring the scalp. Physical pain would be so welcome now, anything to draw his thoughts away from the invisible heartrending hurt. "By God and all the saints, I will find a way free of this coil!" He swallowed hard and drew his hand away, vaguely aware of the bits of skin and blood entombed beneath his nails.

"I am wed to him and all the world's wishing will not undo it. Beyond that I…I love him."

Callum stared at her, feeling as if the floorboards

were seesawing beneath his feet. "You do not! Pity him mayhap but love him you do not."

Her gaze slid away. "I do. I love him."

He caught her gaze and willed her not to look away. "You're lying. I see it in your eyes."

She looked back at him then, her expression so plaintive his heart would have broken were it not in bloody strips already. "My eyes?"

"Aye, you willna use them to look at me." He reached out and touched her cheek. "My brother bears two scars on the inside of his hand, one white and wizened, the other pink and fresh. The first was made as a blood oath between him and Brianna when they pledged themselves to each other as weans, the second made a decade later when first she brought him to her bed. I would bear such a token of you. Whether you love me or not, I would wear your mark to my grave." He drew out his dirk.

"Callum, dinna!" Expression horrified, she reached for his arm. "Because of me, you have borne enough already."

He shrugged her off. Jaw clenched, he stretched out his left forearm. Pinning the elbow to his torso, he slashed as savagely and deeply as he dared. Once, twice, thrice…

"Oh, Callum."

Face aghast, she stared down at the damage. Blood pooled in his palm and spilled through his fingers onto the rushes.

Grounding himself in the pain, he smiled. "Like a rune, your symbol will be my oracle for the rest of my days." He wiped the blood on his kilt and stretched out his hand palm up, revealing the rough-hewn *A*.

"Oh, my lord, what have you done? You bleed too

much." Eyes wide, she tugged at her veil, pulling off the muslin to make of it a makeshift bandage.

He refused to accept it. The free-flowing blood alone was his to release or control. "If I canna have you for my wife, then I'll have nay wife at all. If I canna have your heart, your full heart, then I'll have no heart at all." He caught her hand in his cut one, laced his fingers through hers and squeezed.

"I Callum, Laird of the Frasers, do solemnly swear on mine honor and all that I hold holy to consecrate myself to you in body, mind and soul, forsaking all others for the rest of my earthly days."

She tried pulling away, refusing him, but he wouldn't let her. "Callum, you mustn't. An oath made in blood is a sacred act. Take it back before 'tis too late." She sent him a beseeching look.

He but squeezed her hand tighter, their skin slipping in the slickness. "'Tis done, lady, and live with it I will and most gladly."

And it was done, entirely done. Such a vow, once made, could not be taken back. Nor did he wish to. He'd meant every word. For the first time since Alexander Field had entered his great hall and wreaked havoc upon his happiness, he knew a moment's peace.

A knock sounded outside his door. Breaking hands with Alys, Callum called out, "Who goes there?"

The door creaked slowly open. Milread appeared in the portal, Alasdair in her arms. Her sightless gaze centered on Alys. "The bags are packed and taken below, milady. You asked me to bring the bairn."

Alys nodded. "I did. Thank you." She turned back to Callum. "I thought you would want to say goodbye."

He swallowed hard. "Aye, I do." The sight of Alasdair's cherub's face had the lump blocking Callum's throat building into a boulder. Making sure to hide his bloodied hand behind his back so as not to frighten the boy, he crossed the room, leaned low and kissed the child's plump cheek. "Be a good lad and mind your mam. Papa…I love you."

Alasdair twisted, reaching for him. "Papa! Papa, come!"

Callum drew back. Dividing his gaze between Alys and Alasdair, the full force of his loss hit him. He wasn't only losing his lady but his child, as well. He who had led men into battle and once wrestled a wild boar to the ground with naught but a dirk felt his composure draining away like a tree tapped of its sap.

Before he might shame himself by breaking down, he turned quickly to Milread. "Take the boy and leave us."

For once the old woman offered no argument. She shifted her gaze to Alys. "We will await you below." She turned and carried Alasdair away.

Callum stood at the door. Fixing his gaze on the back of the boy's blond head, he owned he likely would never see him again. He'd never now have the chance to take him to the tilt yard or to the burn to fish or to his council meetings to learn clan ways. He would never now have the chance to see him grow from child to man. Ere now, he hadn't realized how very much he'd been looking forward to doing all those things and more. He hadn't realized how very much he'd been looking forward to being a father.

Throat working, he closed the door and turned back inside. "I would give you something, a gift, before you go."

Like watching Alasdair grow up, the twelve nights of sensual gifts would never happen now. The gift he had in mind was to do with practicality, not pleasure, and he prayed to God she would take it.

She shook her head. "You have given me more than I deserve already."

Rather than waste precious time refuting that claim yet again, he reached down to his belt and unknotted his purse. Freeing it, he held it out. "I would give you this."

She recoiled. "I willna take money from you. Not from you, my lord. It would be too much like..." Though she left the thought unfinished, the allusion to her prostitute past wasn't lost on him.

He closed the distance between them and pressed the purse into her hand. "Then take it for Alasdair. He was almost my son. I will always think of him as such. At least let me have the peace of knowing he suffers no want."

Alys hesitated, biting at her bottom lip, her mother's heart warring with her principles. As he'd hoped, the mother's heart won. "Thank you." She closed her fist over the money. "I should take my leave now. We are packed and...and Alex will not want to lose the light." She made as if to walk past him.

Before she could, he wheeled about, blocking her path. "Before you go, I crave a gift from you."

She stalled in her steps. "My lord?"

"Kiss me, lady. Kiss me true." Anticipating her

protest, he grabbed her wrists, drawing her to him, drawing her close. "Just kisses, only kisses, but let them be kisses I may live off for the rest of my days."

She shook her head, her mouth trembling. "Sweet my lord, once I am gone, there will be ladies aplenty wanting to kiss you."

"I don't want kisses from them. I don't want kisses from any lady save you. So kiss me, Alys. Kiss me fondly. Kiss me farewell. If part we must, then part from me with kisses, kisses I can carry with me to my grave along with this scar."

She hesitated, and then stepped up to him. Slender arms wound about his neck. She drew his head down at the same time lifting her face. Rising up on her toes, she kissed his forehead, the bridge of his nose, and the corners of his mouth. She kissed his jaw, the side of his neck, the curve of his shoulder. Finally she kissed him full on the lips. He opened. For the only time in his memory, she entered him first, her tongue touching his.

"Just kisses, only kisses." Drawing back, she reached for his hand, his hurt hand. He gave it to her—he could deny her nothing, not before and certainly not now. She turned it over, palm up, and bent her head. "Just kisses, only kisses…" Her voice drifted off. She ran her tongue along the trio of cuts, the *A* that would always, always mean *Alys* for him, lapping at the blood, drinking in the sadness, consecrating their shared pain.

She lowered his hand at last. Holding on to his wrist, she fixed her welling gaze upon his and shook her head. "I dinna know how to say goodbye to you." A tear slid down her cheek.

That tear was more precious to Callum than a diamond. She might have a fondness for Field, she might even love the man, but seeing that tear told him she loved him, Callum Fraser, a little, too. She loved him still.

He reached out and caught the crystalline droplet on the edge of his thumb. "Then let us not say goodbye. Let us say 'go safely for now.' Go safely for now, my lady. Whether you love me a little or a lot, whether I may hoard your heart for myself or whether I must share it with another, whether I see you again in this life or only in the shadow land of my dreams matters not. You are forever my lady, my one true love, and aye, my Christmas bride."

5

SO MANY GOODBYES…

Seated atop her palfrey, the gentlest mount Callum's groomsman might find, Alys looked down on Milread, a bawling Alasdair swaddled against her breast. "I shall miss you, Milread. You have been a good and true friend to me."

Standing atop the mounting block, Milread reached up to tweak Alasdair's bootie-covered feet. "Our paths will cross again, wean, and mayhap sooner than you think. This current sorrow will run its course and there will be joy again."

As much as Alys wanted to believe that, she didn't see how it could possibly be so. At present, the prospect of a joyful future seemed as attainable as pixie dust or a moon made entirely of green cheese.

Alasdair pushed against her, protesting the swaddling though they'd yet to set out. She pressed a kiss atop his golden head and shook her head. "Alex is my husband in the eyes of the law and God. The claim he makes upon me is his by right. Beyond that, I loved him once. I loved him true. I gave up everything, my home, my family, my friends, to be with him. And yet now I feel nothing for him beyond pity. How can that be?"

Milread fixed her with a knowing look. "Beyond his face turning from fair to foul, mayhap he has changed less than you might think. You, though, have altered greatly. The girl you once were has grown into a fine, strong woman, a woman loving and wise."

Had Alex always been this way, and she'd simply been too infatuated to notice? It was possible. She'd been so very young then, easily impressed and even more easily led. When he'd insisted they elope and come north even though winter was fast approaching, it had never occurred to her to question him. He'd sworn on his honor to take care of her, and blindly, trustingly she'd followed.

She shook her head, torn between laughter and the terrible desire to scream. "I have never felt less wise in all my life."

"But you are. You are!" Milread grabbed her hand, which still bore Callum's dried blood. "Your eyes are open wide now, all three. You see him for what he is, not for what you once wished he might be. That is wisdom."

Alys let out a bitter laugh. "If so, then it has come too late to do me good."

"We shall see. Mind you, the final rune in your reading was Wyrd, the cosmic void, the gateway to both everything and nothing. The Fates have yet to spin the ending to your story. Much of what drives events is still hidden from our view. All may not yet be lost. In the coming days, mind your inner wisdom for in so doing, you will feel the breath of the gods whispering in your ear."

Alys might have asked more, but Alex walked his mount up to them. "Still goodbying?"

Milread spat upon the cobbles at his horse's hooves.

"My lady is ill at ease on horseback and the distance is too great for her to carry the bairn in the saddle with her. Let her and the bairn be borne in the litter the Fraser provided."

He scowled, his horse pawing the ground. "My wife is not some china doll to be coddled. The sooner she accepts her lot as a foot soldier's wife, the better she will fare."

She snarled. "Your soul matches your face, I see. Were it not for milady and the wean, I would put upon you a curse that would make the smallpox seem mild."

"Milread!"

Horrified, Alys reached down and grabbed for her friend's hand. She wasn't afraid for Alex so much as she was for Milread. Bad luck had a way of bouncing back. She'd never before known the wise woman to ill wish anyone.

Alex scowled, making the puckered lip more pronounced. "In England we burn witches. What a pity we're not there now." He shifted his gaze to Alys. "We have a long journey ahead, my love, and I am eager to be on my way."

She nodded. "I will follow you anon."

Seemingly satisfied, he nodded and turned his horse in the direction of the gate.

Alasdair burst into tears. "Kit-ty. Want Kit-ty!"

Alex huffed. "What is he bawling about now?"

"He wants his cat," Alys answered. Addressing Alasdair in a soothing voice she said, "Dinna fret, sweeting. We'll send someone to fetch your kitty cat before we go."

Alex scowled. "You'll do no such thing."

Wondering why her husband must be so difficult,

she lifted her face from Alasdair's reddened one. "Why ever not?"

"I loathe cats. I refuse to have the scurrilous beasts about me. God only knows what diseases they carry."

Though she'd spent the hour since leaving Callum praying to the Virgin to be a more biddable wife, Alys felt her temper rise. "That's ridiculous. Cat is my responsibility. I have tamed him and fed him and made a pet of him. Alasdair loves him dearly. If we don't bring him with us, what do you suggest I do with him?"

He shrugged. "You may drown the creature for all I care."

"Drown him!" She drew back. "You would murder an innocent animal and deprive our son of his pet? Is it not enough that he must give up the only father he has ever known?"

Alex fisted his leather-gloved hands. "I am the lad's sire. I and no other. The sooner he learns that, the better it will go with him." He urged his horse past them.

Milread reached up and squeezed her hand. "Dinna fret, wean. I will care for the wee beastie until you can reclaim him."

Alys felt her shoulders fall. "Thank you, Milread, only I can't say when that would be. Alex is determined to take us to England. What he means to do once we arrive there, he hasna said. Rejoin his lord's army, I suppose."

She heartily hoped he would. A soldier's life was spent largely away from home. If she must live out her days as Alex's wife, mayhap she might be spared having to pass too very many of them in his physical company.

From across the courtyard, she caught Alex beckoning her and sighed. "I must go. Pray give my love to Brianna."

She'd planned to attend Brie at her lying-in and to help Milread with the delivery. Now she would never see her friend again or come to know her unborn babe. So many goodbyes, so many dear friends to whom she must bid farewell.

She glimpsed a glimmering on Milread's shrunken cheeks. "Why, Milread, are those tears I see?"

"Of course not," the crone snapped. "I am an old woman. The cold stings my eyes."

"Then my eyes must be stinging, as well." She reached down and squeezed her friend's hand. "I hadn't thought I'd have to say so many goodbyes today and at Christmastide, no less." She gathered the horse's reins and moved forward.

Just kisses, only kisses...

She forced herself not to look back. How she wished she might have found the courage to carve Callum's initial, a *C* into her own palm. Were it not for having to explain the wound to Alex, she would have done so. As it was, it had required all her willpower not to draw out the jewel-handled dirk Callum had given her as a present and do the same violence to her own hand. A scar would have been such a fitting keepsake of their beautiful seven months together, for despite what she'd said earlier, she couldn't believe the wound of losing him would ever truly heal.

Tears striking her cheeks, she crossed the courtyard to the bridged gate. On the cusp of passing over, she couldn't help herself. She weakened. She looked back.

She honed in on the eastern tower and the uppermost arched window belonging to the laird's solar, Callum's solar. Gaze straining, she still couldn't see whether or not he watched from within, but selfish woman that she was, she liked to think he did. In case he did, she raised her hand in farewell and silently said the words she hadn't dared utter to his face.

Goodbye, my Callum. Though I willna be able to share that lifetime of Christmases with you after all, I swear to keep you in my heart, you and only you, for the rest of my days.

So THIS IS WHAT it meant to lose.

Kneeling on the velvet-covered bench before his family crypt that eve, Callum realized he'd never before lost, not really. He'd always wondered privately what it might feel like. Ere now, he'd been a darkened version of the golden boy, the flawed hero, the winner. Whether the contest was caber tossing or wenching, he'd always been the front-runner, the leader of the pack, the victor whose only concern was in what manner to collect his spoils. Lazy lout though he must have been even in the womb, still he'd somehow managed to be born a full few minutes before his twin, cinching for himself the title of laird. For someone who'd always applied himself so very little, he'd enjoyed an enormous bounty of success. He'd never expected to experience loss firsthand.

But now he'd lost in a very big, very personal way. He'd lost Alys, not for an hour or a day but for the totality of their earthly lives. No amount of praying could begin to alleviate the pain.

He turned over his bandaged hand, the fabric of Alys's veil clotted with his blood. The *A* he'd carved into his flesh would honor her until the day he was laid in his grave. Wanting to see it, he unsheathed his dirk, thinking to cut the cloth away. But staring down at the candlelight glancing off the blade, temptation of a different sort seized him. He played the blade about his wrist and thought how easy it all might suddenly be. One slash, sharp and sure, would secure the deed and afterward, the final, coveted peace.

"Callum Fraser, drop that dirk—now!"

Startled, he let go of the knife. It clattered to the stone floor. He followed it, falling forward onto the flagging. He bowed his head and slammed his fisted hands into the sockets of his fast-filling eyes.

Beside him the kneeling bench creaked. A warm hand settled on his back. Callum turned his head and met the kind eyes of Father Fearghas, his parents' priest, his priest now. A burly man of middling years and yeoman stock, the good father had tutored Callum and his brother in Latin and Greek, geography and ancient history. Scholarly Ewan was the favored one, of course. Then again, putting toads in his tutor's confessional and painting curse words on the back of his cassock were hardly the ways to curry favor. Sputtering and scarlet-faced, the priest had regularly predicted the damnation of Callum's soul. Like all pranksters, Callum had found his victim's suffering hilarious at the time. Now he wondered if his misdeeds weren't finally catching up with him.

"Talk to me, my son."

Callum hesitated. Though he'd known Father Fearghas all his life, still he had a powerful distrust of holy men, which he found difficult to move past. When he'd first become laird, he'd been tricked into making a pilgrimage to the monastery of St. Simeon by Brother Bartholomew, who'd scourged his back—and stolen a scrap of his plaid, which he'd passed on to Brianna's traitorous advisor, Duncan. Soon after Duncan had killed the lady laird's first husband and planted the plaid in the murdered man's hand. Predictably a blood feud had followed. Fortunately all had ended well. The feud was healed, the traitorous Duncan dispatched, and Brianna and Ewan united in holy matrimony with a bairn soon to be born. And yet Callum's face still heated to think of how easily he'd been duped. That encounter had been his humbling and the beginning of his reformation. He'd realized he must cease living for pleasure and start being a chieftain in deed as well as name.

And then he'd met Alys. With her at his side, steering him with her simple wisdom and quiet strength, he'd felt as though he could move mountains.

And now that dream was dead.

In desperation he blurted out, "I dinna ken how to go on without her." He smacked a hand to his brow, clammy with sweat though the sanctuary was cold.

Father Fearghas didn't hesitate. "Day by day, hour by hour, and minute by minute just as she is doing."

"I'd rather be dead."

The priest grabbed him by the shoulders. "You think ending your life will bring you peace but it willna. Do you want to close out your days with your soul unshriven and your body buried at a crossroads grave?"

Callum shrugged. "I scarcely care how they end so long as end they do."

Father Fearghas screwed his face into a frown. "And what of Alys? Does that poor, brave lady not have a surfeit of sorrows already without you adding to them?"

Callum broke down. "Father, help me. I don't know what to do, how to go on without her." He who'd never before humbled himself had done so twice in fewer than twenty-four hours. "Mayhap I should take vows."

Father Fearghas tossed back his tonsured head and laughed. The chapel filled with his guffaws. Finishing, he swiped at his watery eyes.

Callum balled his hands into fists. "I pour out my soul's sorrows and you dare mock me! You, a priest!"

Father Fearghas shook his head. There was no trace of apology in his reddened face. "Priest or no, how can I help myself? In my fifty-odd years, I've never known a man less suited for the collar than you, Callum Fraser. Your energies are best directed to the temporal world. There is no reproach in that for the Almighty Himself fashioned you so." He cocked his head to the side. "Is that dripping I hear?"

They both looked down. Callum saw that his makeshift bandage was soaked through to sopping. Blood splashed the stones.

The good father swallowed hard. "That hand of yours wants for tending." He stood and helped Callum to his feet. For a little man, he was both burly and strong. "Come, my lord, let us get you fed and tended and bedded. After a night's rest, matters will look brighter on the morrow."

Callum tried pulling away. He opened his mouth to proclaim he didn't need anyone's help but before he could, the chapel pivoted, and then seesawed. He sagged against the stout little body which, he realized, was holding him up. When God humbled a man, it seemed He did so all at once.

"Draw it mild, my lord." Father Fearghas firmed his hold. "For this night at least, put you in the Lord's hands—and mine."

ALYS AND ALEX PASSED most of their day's ride in silence, Alys deep in thought as she struggled to hold her seat. Alasdair fussed frequently, not that she blamed him. Arms and back aching, she felt fussy herself. She lanced a look to Alex riding ahead and felt her resentment rise. More than a horse's breadth separated them. She'd been staring at his horse's hind side for hours and though she had no real desire for his company, his lack of care grated. Since they'd left Callum's castle, not once had he offered to take their son from her or to help her in any way. Harkening back to their trip north, she realized he'd not been much more solicitous of her comfort then. Despite her pregnancy, he'd pushed her to ride hard. More than once, he'd shown annoyance when she'd had to stop to relieve herself or be sick. Now that Alasdair was born, he was hardly showing himself to be a tender father. Thinking of how wonderful Callum was to them both, recalling the hurt look on his handsome face when she'd lied and said she loved Alex, she felt tears squeeze out of her eyes. It might be the second day of Christmastide, but never had she felt less hope or joy in all her life.

A dust cloud from ahead signaled another rider was fast approaching. She tensed. Alex hadn't only refused the litter for her. He'd also refused safe escort to the border, folly indeed. The open road was a dangerous place but particularly so on a holy day when the lesser thoroughfares were deserted. A couple with a baby would make easy prey for bandits or worse. She felt inside Alasdair's swaddling, checking for the money purse she'd hidden there, and then reached for her dirk.

The rider overtook them and slowed to a canter. Seeing that he wore the MacLeod colors, she relaxed and sheathed her knife.

He touched his forelock to her and addressed himself to Alex. "Good master, can you point me the way to the Fraser fortress? I've a most urgent message for the laird there."

Alys spoke up. "We have just come from there. You are not so verra far away. If you retrace your path to the northern highway and then head due east, you may make Beauly before nightfall."

Relief washed over his young features. "I thank you." He urged his mount forward.

Alys reached out and caught his sleeve. "Halt. Before you depart, is something amiss?"

He jerked free. "I must be on my way."

"I used to wait upon the MacLeod. I am her former handmaid, Alys. If some ill has befallen my lady, I would know of it."

In the twilight, she saw his eyes widen to the whites. "The same Lady Alys who is to wed the Fraser?"

"I am. I was." Avoiding Alex's gaze, she said, "Tell me, please."

"The MacLeod's pains started late last night."

The news slashed at Alys's heart. Brianna so wanted this baby. And poor Ewan, he would go mad if any harm befell his lady. "But she is not due for almost two more months."

"Aye, hence my haste. Lord Ewan set me to fetch the witch woman, Milread, and bring her back."

"Be on your way then and Godspeed."

He broke into a gallop, raising clumps of dirt and clouds of dust.

Alex drew up beside her. "If you are thinking what I think you are, then think again. We are bound for England. You are my wife. Your duty is to me."

Alys drew a deep breath. Heart pounding, still she measured her words. "Aye, I am your wife. But I am also a mother and, in this case, a friend. Brianna needs me. I must go to her. I will go to her."

"Alys, I'm commanding you. Stay you here."

Alys turned her horse's head and set her course for Skye and the MacLeod lands.

STANDING OUTSIDE his laird's solar Father Fearghas marveled at how a mere hour could alter one's perspective, in the present case, his. Up until an hour ago, he'd not been overly fond of Callum Fraser. Far from fond, he'd harbored a dislike of his former pupil, now brash young laird.

He'd been but a young man himself, a newly collared priest, when he'd first come into the Fraser household to serve the previous laird as chaplain. Once the twins, Callum and Ewan, attained a certain age, tutoring them had become one of his primary duties. Ewan was the scholar, the sensitive one, the brother whom Father Fearghas would have chosen to be laird. Mayhap it was the contrast between pupils that caused him to paint Callum so black. Looking back, he allowed that in the main, the boy's misdeeds were more capricious than cruel. Still, Fearghas had spent many a night on his knees praying for the strength to overcome his dislike. That prayer had been answered this last hour in a way that he would not have wished on his very worst enemy.

The girl, Alys, was good for him. With her gentleness and unassuming presence, she had succeeded in reaching Callum where so many others, himself included, had failed. It was enough to make a man such as himself question his faith.

"He sleeps."

Lost to his thoughts, Fearghas started. The witch woman, Milread, drew up beside him. Blind as she was reputed to be, it was a marvel how easily she moved about.

Gathering himself, he asked, "How does he fare?"

She shrugged. "The hand will heal with time. Of his heart, I am less sure."

He nodded. The day's doings had torn the young laird asunder. He was battered in both body and soul. A broken heart didn't mend overnight, but a grief-wracked body could greatly benefit from the healing power of sleep.

Her cracked voice broke into his thoughts. "I leave at

first light. The MacLeod has called me home. A messenger arrived a while ago to say that her pains have come on."

Fearghas stared at her, marveling at her unnatural lack of concern. "If you're her midwife, shouldn't you set out at once?"

She tossed back her grizzled head and cackled, looking every whit the unholy creature she was. "A surfeit of fine holy-day fare sets ill on a pregnant belly."

"You canna say so for certain without examining her."

She snorted. "Och, I ken things, priest, that you with your collar and frock canna begin to mind."

Rather than engage in pointless argument, he said, "I too am leaving on the morrow...to visit my sister, Enid. She is the anchoress at the Church of St. Andrew in Portree. That is where the Lady Alys was first wed, is it not?"

"Aye, it is." Milread broke into a crooked grin. "You go on a fishing expedition, do you, priest?"

He hesitated, and then nodded. "When the Almighty closes one door, he almost always leaves open a window—and a great many flock to my sister's cell window. Beyond that, she has the parish priest's ear. If there was the slightest irregularity with the proceedings, anything that might be brought to bear in a case for annulment, she will know of it."

She fixed him with her blind, steady stare. "You go to a great deal of trouble for a master you dislike."

He didn't deny it. "For many a year, I looked upon him as my cross to bear. There were times when I came close to hating him."

"And now?"

He leaned his aching back against the stone wall. "I'd do a'most anything to see his wounded heart healed and his love returned to him."

He'd thought she might mock him but instead she nodded. "As I would so for the Lady Alys. I've nay known her long, but I love her well." She gazed ahead. "We're nay so verra different, you and I. We both trade in belief, you in your One God and me in my ancient deities and magick. I minister to those with sick minds and bodies and you to sick souls. Were we to join forces, it might be that both our purposes would be better served."

"Mayhap we already have." Fearghas pushed away from the wall. "For now, I'm to bed." He started down the corridor to the stairs, Milread keeping pace beside.

Coming to the end, they parted ways. Fearghas couldn't think why but suddenly he was moved to say, "Go with God, my daughter."

Looking up at him, she smiled her broken smile. "May Odin and Frigga speed you on your journey, priest."

6

By the advent of the first evening, Alys felt as though she'd survived a trial by fire and only narrowly. In the course of their first day's journey, Alex's complaining easily outstripped Alasdair's. It was as if she had two babes in tow rather than one. Worried for Brianna, she wished to ride for a few more hours whilst they still had the light, but Alex wouldn't hear of it. He insisted they stop for the night. In the end she relented but only because Alasdair needed to be changed and fed. It wasn't until they'd dismounted in the inn yard that Alex announced he hadn't any coin.

"You've nay money!" Rocking a fussing Alasdair in her aching arms, she whirled on him. "Then why did you insist we stop?"

Looping the reins over the tethering post, he slanted a sly look her way. "Don't be coy with me, Alys. Contrary to what you seem to think of me, I am no fool. I saw the way the Scottish scum looked at you as though the sun rises and sets between your thighs. He wouldn't have let you leave his stronghold penniless."

She dropped her gaze to Alasdair, glad he was as yet too young to comprehend his sire's crudity. "You imagine things."

"Do I now?" Smiling, he strode over to her. "If that is so, you can always pay for our bed and board in other ways." His reached out, his gloved fingers trailing the side of her face.

Alys smacked his hand away, telling herself the remark was but tasteless teasing. So far as she knew, Alex was unaware of how she'd kept herself and their son. Sick abed in England, how could he know?

"If need be, we will sleep in the barn and sup on fallen apples first."

Alasdair lifted his head from her breast. "Alasdair hung-ar-y. Hung-ar-y!" Tears spilled from his blue eyes onto his baby cheeks, the sight tearing at her heart.

"Suit yourself." Expression smug, Alex shrugged and walked away, toward the inn which was little bigger than a crofter's thatched cottage.

In the end, he won his way. Alys produced the purse. Standing within the sloped alcove, she meant to discreetly dole out the required coins once they'd negotiated the price. Before she could, Alex snatched the purse from her. He shook it, sending coins jingling.

"That money belongs to me. It is to be used for Alasdair's keeping." She grabbed for the pouch, but he only laughed and held it higher.

He cocked his head and regarded her as though she were a child to whom he must patiently explain things. "You forget yourself, Alys. You are my wife. Aside from the clothes on your back, nothing belongs to you."

Once she might have been chastened, but she was almost two years older than she'd been when he'd left. In many ways, she'd lived a lifetime since then. She opened her mouth to reply that she'd kept herself and her son in clothes and food without his help when the innkeepers, a husband and wife, came out to greet them. Catching sight of the plump purse being waved about, they exchanged bright-eyed glances. Minutes later, they were ushered into a low-ceiling room above the stairs, for which Alys was sure they greatly overpaid.

Alex cost them dearly at dinner, too. Ignoring her imploring looks, he insisted on bespeaking the finest fare the inn had to offer. Again the couple exchanged jubilant glances. No doubt it was a long time since they'd hosted a guest so free with "his" coin.

Weary and heartsick, Alys made do with bread and cheese. Hungry though she was, chewing and swallowing even that seemed an effort. Throughout the meal, Alex scarcely looked at her or their son, which suited her well enough. She fed Alasdair choice bits from the platter of roast pig Alex gorged himself upon and bespoke a cup of goat's milk. Before long, her little boy's eyelids drifted closed and his head sagged against her breast.

Alex lifted the flagon of costly French Bordeaux he alone had drained and clanged it upon the table. "More wine and make it sharp." Beneath his breath, he muttered, "Scots slattern."

Alys couldn't be certain if he was speaking of the innkeeper's wife or her, and she was far too weary and dispirited to care. She waited until the wife had collected the empty vessel and moved out of earshot before grabbing his goblet away.

"Alex, what are you about?"

Wine streamed down the puckered side of his scarred mouth. He levered one elbow upon the table and swayed toward her. "Why, being of good cheer on Christmastide. Is that some crime?"

Reaching for patience, Alys answered, "That money must last us God alone knows how long. The journey to London will take weeks, and you still havena said what manner of employment you mean to pursue once we arrive."

He shrugged. "You never used to be such a shrew. Mind what a merry adventure we had when last we came north?"

He reached for her hand but she snatched it away. "As I recall that *merry adventure* ended with me breeding and abandoned. We were children then. We're grown now. We have a son to think of."

He slanted his heavy-lidded gaze toward Alasdair, thankfully sleeping in her arms. So far as she could tell, it was the first time he'd deigned to acknowledge their son since they'd set out that morning. Thinking of what a wonderful father Callum was, she felt the familiar lump lodge in her throat. Her lost love was Alasdair's loss, as well.

She slid off the backless bench to her feet, Alasdair in her arms. "I'm putting our son to bed and myself, as well."

His mottled face twisted. "I did not give you my leave."

"I didna ask for it." She turned to go but not before picking up the purse he'd carelessly cast upon the table. They had been robbed blind enough for one night.

On her way to the stairs, she intercepted the

innkeeper's wife returning with the replenished wine. "Good mistress, let that wine be the last you serve him unless you wish to do so freely." She held up the purse.

Predictably the woman's expression went from glad to glum. She shuffled past Alys with far less spring in her step.

Climbing the creaking wooden steps, Alys knew that beyond feeling weary and put out, she felt relieved. Alex's drunkenness and squandering, disgusting as they were, had purchased her a night of peace. For this eve at least, she and Alasdair would sleep alone.

Reaching their room, she bolted the door from within and laid Alasdair down in the center of the bed. He still had not awakened. The very picture of baby beauty with his mussed blond curls and sweetly curved features, he curled onto his side, suckling his thumb.

Her heart squeezed in on itself as it was wont to do at such times. Before meeting Callum, Alasdair had been the center of her universe. Now that Callum was lost to her, so must her child become again. So long as she had her son, she would find the strength to go on. Too tired to bother with undressing, she laid herself down on the straw-stuffed mattress beside him, pulled the thin coverlet over them both, and snuggled him to her.

She must have fallen asleep at once. She awakened to the cock's crowing in the courtyard beneath her window. Cradled in the crook of her arm, Alasdair slept still. Her poor little lad must be exhausted. Given that they were the inn's only guests, she left him to his rest and came downstairs. She wasn't surprised to find Alex still slumped over the table. Lying facedown on the swine carcass, his sleeve sopping the spillage from the overturned wine goblet, he made a lamentable first morning's sight.

Alys sighed. She needed to find food so that Alasdair might break his fast but before she did, she would greatly benefit from splashing some water on her face. Catching the eye of the sallow-faced maid mopping around them, she bade the girl good morning and bespoke a bucket of washing water.

Scowling, the maid continued to push the mop about the dusty boards. "Clean water's a ducat."

"A ducat for a pail of water?" They must have sized her and Alex up for easy marks, indeed. Reining in her annoyance, Alys thought for a moment. "Nay worries." She walked over to the pail of brown water, grabbed hold of the handle, and carried it over to the table where Alex still snored.

"Rise and shine." She hoisted the pail and upturned it over Alex's head.

He came awake, sputtering and snorting. Cursing a blue streak, he shook himself, spraying droplets like a dog emerging from wading.

Alys sighed heavily. She righted the empty bucket and walked outside to refill it from the well. Once they reached the ferry at Mallaig that would carry them from the mainland to Skye, they had another few hours' ride at most. So long as they left within the hour, they might reach the MacLeod Castle whilst it was yet light.

Still, it promised to be a long day.

SHIVERING IN THE QUEUE outside his sister, Enid's anchorage, Father Fearghas realized that his bossy senior sibling had become a most celebrated personage. Like the many others who'd come for an audience with the anchoress, he'd waited in the cold for the past hour. With each visitor who stepped up to her cell window, he'd hoped the visit would be shorter than the previous and each time he was disappointed. If anything, the time spent seemed to lengthen with each visitor received. Enid's voice crackled above the collective whispering, weeping and shuffling feet. Even as a child, she'd been a notorious chatterbox. Apparently little had changed. She chatted and joked, dispensed advice and the occasional prayer as if she had all the time in the world while he stamped his feet to keep feeling in the toes.

His turn finally came. He stepped up to the window and peered down. Enid's wimpled face came into view, plumper than he remembered.

Her small eyes lit. "Why Fergie, I havena seen you in donkey's years."

He hated it when she called him Fergie.

"What brings you here, little brother?"

He hated it when she called him little brother.

Minded of his mission, he put on a smile. "Does a brother need a reason to pay his own dear sister a Christmastide call?"

The last time he'd visited was two years ago, the day she'd taken her final vows. Heading the processional from the church sanctuary, she'd approached the grim rituals of enclosure and entombment with all the gaiety of a bride. Now he understood why. Peering past her, he saw that along with the crucifix, narrow bed and altar of his memory, the cell was filled with books! Bookshelves lined all four walls, including the windowless one shared with the church. More books stood in stacks on the floor alongside a pile of parcels. Owing to two more windows, a squint through which she could receive communion and other offices of the church, and an attendant's window through which food and linens and refuse were passed, the room was sunny, positively cheerful, the light perfect for reading. Fearghas experienced a startling and decidedly un-Christian stab of sibling envy. With people flocking to see her and hanging on her every word, no chores to do, and endless hours for reading, clever Enid had landed herself in the catbird seat.

Her gaze narrowed. "I ken that look upon your face. It puts me in mind of when we were weans and you were forever after me to surrender my share of the Christmastide comfits."

Fearghas recalled the bullying being the other way around but rather than reprise their childhood hostilities, he admitted, "There is a matter on which I seek your help, a delicate matter for which I will require your complete discretion."

She smiled smugly. "I thought as much. Spill the barley, brother. I have supplicants still to receive. Only come closer. I canna hear you otherwise."

Fearghas hesitated. Fighting a frown, he got down on his knees, stiff from decades of genuflecting. Not wanting to be eavesdropped upon, he glanced back over his shoulder. The zigzagging line had grown like

a dragon's tail. For the first time he noticed what he
had not before. Everyone who waited seemed to be
holding some item of wrapped food. That's when it
struck him.

Enid was exacting payment for her prayers!

Fuming, he turned back to her. "You should be
ashamed of yourself, using prayers to prey upon people
and put up your pantry. Along with your Anchoress's
Rule of Life, you would do well to mind the vows you
took before it, notably poverty!"

Rather than repent, Enid rolled her eyes. "Och,
Fergie, you always were a spoiler. If you've come to
piddle on my pageant, then be on your way. But before
you go, what have *you* brought me?"

Minded of his own vows, humility especially, he
reached inside his cloak for the pouch he'd all but forgotten. "Marzipan. The Fraser employs a verra fine con-
fectioner." Grudgingly he slid it through the bars.

"I do love a good marzipan." A short-fingered hand
snatched the gift inside. She pulled on the cord, dug a
hand inside the pouch and popped several of the sweets
into her mouth. Chomping, she asked, "So what is the
nature of this 'delicate matter' that you must journey all
this way to put it to me?"

Holding his voice to a high whisper, he recounted
what had taken place in the Fraser's great hall on Christmas Day. Finishing, he admitted, "I'd hoped there might
be some irregularity in the proceedings, some fluke that
might render the marriage invalid or at least provide a
case for having it annulled."

"Aye, I do remember it, for 'twas just before my enclosure." She set the empty bag aside and sucked the sugar from her fingers. "Sorry to disappoint, little brother, but if we're minded of the same couple, they were wedded proper. An Outlander, fair-faced and fair-haired with a soldier's bearing. The bride was Scots, though, only judging from her speech, a Lowlander."

Fearghas's heart sank like a millstone. After parting ways with Milread, he'd spent most of the remaining night on his knees praying for a Christmas miracle. He'd had such hopes that such a marvel might materialize. It had taken but one sentence from his sister to dash those hopes upon the frozen ground.

He was about to rise and bid Enid goodbye when she added, "I wouldna say she was fair. On the bony side, if you ask me."

Fearghas hesitated. Enid's kirtle's stretching tight across her broad girth spoke to her fondness for food. What she considered bony might well be a normal female physique.

"The Lady Alys is petite and slender, but I wouldna say she is bony." He waited, scarcely daring to breathe.

Enid shrugged. "In truth, it was the plucked forehead and painted face I couldn't abide. I ken 'tis the fashion and yet too many women these days follow it to the extreme and spoil their natural looks."

He hesitated again. "I am of course no expert in these matters, but I do not believe the Lady Alys applies cosmetics of any kind. But then a face as fair and fresh as hers needs no artifice."

"Fair and fresh?" Enid chortled. "I may have given up life outside these cell walls but you, brother, must be giving up sight. The bride I saw was more in the way of youngish than young, as a head of boiled cabbage might be compared to a salad of tender greens if you ken my meaning."

Suspicion tickled the corners of his mind, ushering in a cautious hope. "I begin to wonder if we are speaking of the same lady. Tell me, was the marriage recorded, the names and date entered into the parish book?"

"Of course, I'll have you know this is a very proper parish. Births, baptisms, weddings and deaths are always recorded."

"Do you think I might have a look for myself?"

She shrugged. "I don't see why not. I can speak to the priest, Father Seumas, on your behalf. He is a great friend of mine."

Fearghas hadn't expected her to come around so easily, without any bartering whatsoever. Watching her step down from her stool and waddle over to the attendant's window, he felt a niggling guilt, wondering if mayhap he'd been over-harsh in judgment.

Three sharp raps brought the little novice nun hopping to attention. He couldn't make out their hushed voices but a minute or two later, Enid returned.

"Sister Cynthia will take you to see the priest after vespers." She passed a folded sheet of foolscap through the window bars.

"Thank you." He took the paper. "What is this?"

"My marketing list. You should have sufficient time to go into town and fetch me my things before your interview."

He unfolded the paper and perused the long list of

items. Lifting his gaze, he glared down at her. "Do you never do anything for the sheer goodness of it?"

She snorted. "Do you?"

He drew back, offended. "I am a man of the cloth. The immortal souls of a laird and his entire household are daily entrusted to my care. Unlike yours, my word is beyond question, my behavior beyond reproach. Why, even the purity of my spirit touches on the sublime."

She rolled her eyes and jerked her head to indicate the world beyond him. "Look about you to all those people still waiting. Some of them come for prayers, some for advice, and still others to pass the time of day with someone with whom they can talk. But in the main, every man, woman and child standing in that queue comes here for hope. If a slab of bacon or a loaf of sugar buys them the hope to go on another day, do you nay ken the bargain well met? Everyone needs a little hope, Fergie. Did you not come here seeking it yourself?"

She burst out laughing, the cackling putting him in mind of Milread. Mayhap the crone had the right of it after all. Christian or Pagan, follower of the One True God or a diaspora of deities, people weren't so very different after all.

"I SEE NOW why gluttony is accounted one of the Seven Deadly Sins," Brianna said the following morning, pulling a face. "I hope to never look upon another gooseberry tart again. I feel so verra foolish for causing such a hubbub."

The MacLeod lay atop the massive four-poster bed propped against banked pillows, her belly making a mountain of the covers, the christening smock she'd given up on embroidering abandoned in her lap. "The pains cut so sharp, I was sure the bairn must be early."

Alys looked up from the shirt she was stitching for Brianna's babe. Thanks to Callum's generosity, her own son didn't need more clothing or indeed more of anything. She, however, desperately needed to keep busy.

"Dinna berate yourself, Brie. How were you to know? You've nay carried a bairn before."

Even though the danger had been false, still Alys couldn't be sorry she'd come. Alex, on the other hand, couldn't wait to leave. Since their arrival the previous evening, he'd scarcely drawn breath before he'd begun bullying her to set out again. That it was Christmas, and the first he'd spent with his son, seemed not to matter to him at all. Were it not for Brianna's obvious favor, he would have forced the issue, Alys was sure. Fortunately for her, they were in the MacLeod's stronghold and relatively isolated on the Isle of Skye. Had they been on the mainland, she wouldn't have put it past him to throw her and Alasdair across his saddle and bear them away. Still, eager as he was, she didn't believe she could put him off for more than another day or two. As he never tired of pointing out, he was her lord and master.

Brianna nodded. "I confess I am not used to lying about idle, and I am not as clever with my needle as are you. I ought not to complain and yet I can't help it. The waiting weighs heavy on me."

Alys nodded. She well remembered the feeling. "Once you hold him or her in your arms, the waiting and discomfort will seem but a trifling price to pay."

She smiled, thinking back to how the midwife in Portree had cut the cord and laid a newly born Alasdair upon her breast. Exhausted and frightened though she'd been, still it had been a most wondrous moment. She'd hoped to experience such a miracle again by bearing Callum's child but like all her other dreams, that too must die.

Brianna settled intense green eyes upon her. "Your bravery shames me."

Puzzled, Alys said, "My bravery?"

Brie nodded. "Aye, when I think of how you birthed and cared for Alasdair in a foreign land all on your own, your bravery shames me."

Alys felt the tips of her ears heat. Even after seven months of Callum's courtliness and consideration, compliments still sometimes brought out her shyness. For the future, though, fielding praise should present no problem. Alex treated her as more of a possession than a person. Now that he'd gotten her away from Callum, the tolerance he'd shown her on their first night together seemed to be fast fading.

She shrugged and looked down. "As mothers, as women, we do as we must in the best way we may contrive."

Brie arched a brow. "And this husband of yours, does he do the best he can contrive?"

Alys felt her shoulders droop. "Nay, my lady, I fear that he does not." Since arriving the day before and privately telling Brianna and Ewan her sad news, she'd done her best to put on a brave face for her friends. But it was hard, so very hard.

Brianna levered herself up on her elbows. "Might it help to talk the matter through?"

Miserable, Alys shook her head. "What is there to talk of? I am wed, the deed is done and there is no undoing it."

Brie nodded. "I too was wed once against my wishes, to my cousin Donald. And yet only look how my circumstances have altered and in not even a year."

Alys allowed it was so. "And yet you were widowed, my lady. I fear if I think upon your tale overmuch, I may be tempted to wish myself the same, and that I cannot let myself do. Regardless of whom I love, Alex is still my husband and Alasdair's father."

"And what of Callum?"

Unable to meet Brie's gaze, Alys looked away. "Before I left, I told him I loved Alex after all."

"Oh, Alys, you didna!"

Alys sighed. "Aye, I did. I thought to spare him further pain, to make it easier for him to move on with his life but now…" She put down her needlework and sank her head in her hands.

From across the room the bed creaked. Footfalls made their way through the rushes toward her. Brie's scent, rosemary mingled with mint, enfolded her like an embrace.

Her friend's hand found her back. "Do you think he believed you?"

Alys lifted her head and looked up into Brie's face. There she saw no judgment, only concern and a friend's unconditional caring. "If you'd seen the hurt in his eyes when he looked at me, I think he must have, at least a little."

"You must set this right, Alys. Callum deserves to know how you truly feel about him. You owe him that much and yourself, as well." Brie's tone was gentle but firm. "Whatever happens from here on, you cannot leave with this lie standing between you."

Alys sighed. Brie spoke true. Honesty was the best way, the only way. Had she followed that maxim sooner, her life might have followed a straighter, smoother course. When she'd found herself pregnant with Alasdair, her first thought had been to go to her parents and brave her father's anger. Instead she'd let Alex play upon her fears and persuade her to run away with him. She'd tossed her old frock in the mill stream to make it seem as if she'd drowned. At the time, she told herself it would be better for her family, less painful, to think her dead. The other morning with Callum she'd once again employed a lie to make matters better—and once again she'd but made them worse.

Brie broke into her thoughts. "I recall a young woman, wise beyond her years, telling me that our earthly lives amount to but a teardrop in time and that if we do not love one another truly and well whilst we are here, there is little point in living at all. That wise woman was you, Alys. Do you remember that day?"

Alys met her friend's gaze, the lump lodging in her throat making it hard to do more than nod. "Aye, I do."

"Not so verra long ago, I was about to let Ewan go free without confessing that I loved him. I was proud then, but beyond my pride was a terrible fear of being hurt again. Had I not listened to your wise words and taken them to heart, Ewan would be back upon Fraser lands and I would be here—alone. And that would be a terrible tragedy, do you not think?" Brie's hand covered Alys's shoulder. "You are gifted with a rare wisdom and a loving heart. In this instance it isna your head but your heart that holds the answer—and there is only one answer, Alys. You must tell Callum the truth."

Alys didn't trust herself to speak. Acknowledging she'd done wrong was one thing, finding the courage to make it right quite another. If she admitted the true depth of her feelings, what was to stop either of them from committing a far greater sin, a sin from which there was no coming back?

"You will think on what I have said?" Brie pressed.

Alys found her voice and nodded. "Aye, I will."

CHRISTMAS HAD COME AT LAST!

Father Fearghas stared down at the open parish records ledger, half afraid to credit the proof of his eyes. Beside the neatly written date, "April 14, Year of Our Lord 1458," the name *Alexander Field* was penned in a decidedly less tidy yet still decipherable hand. On the line beneath were the initials of his bride: *MG*.

Whoever MG was, she was most certainly not Lady Alys.

A knock sounded outside the door. Fearghas started. The parish priest, Father Seumas, gave the call to enter.

A young priest poked his tonsured head inside. He touched his forelock to Fearghas and then turned to Father Seumas. "I crave your pardon, Father, but 'tis the tanner's wife. She is on her deathbed and sent her son to fetch you so that she may receive the last rites."

The priest let out a put-upon sigh. "Verra well, tell him I will come anon." He waited for the novice to take his leave before turning back to Fearghas. Lowering his voice to a confidential whisper, he explained, "The woman takes to her deathbed at least monthly. She craves attention from her husband. Unfortunately, he is more interested in the innkeeper's comely daughter. Still I must go. You will forgive me?"

Father Fearghas nodded with enthusiasm. Truly the Divine worked in mysterious ways. "Of course, I comprehend completely. Pray and do as you must. I will be but a moment or two at most."

Already rising, Father Seumas nodded. "I thank you for your understanding. Pray take as long as you like. When you are finished, pull yonder bell and someone will come and fetch back the book."

Father Fearghas nodded. "Of course, of course…"

Left to his devices, he felt sweat break out upon his face, several droplets striking the page. He dashed an arm across his forehead lest he obliterate the precious, evidentiary ink.

It was wrong of him, he knew, and yet considering his action would be in the service of a higher power, was it so *terribly* wrong? Once he returned to Castle Fraser and delivered his news to Callum, he would be sure and do proper penance: say sufficient Hail Marys, don a hair shirt, maybe even flagellate himself a time or two for good measure. But he couldn't afford to pause and consider the consequences now. The moment called for bold action, gallant deeds, fearless sacrifice…

He rent the page from the register, closed the book and ran.

IT WAS IN READING *The Pardoner's Tale* later that afternoon that inspiration struck Brianna. In Chaucer's comical yarn, the priest passed off pigs' bones as saints' relics and sold "indulgences" to the gullible, all while preaching against greed. Amusing as the story was, it was also a reminder that people and circumstances were not always what they seemed.

Closing the book, she studied Alys. The girl had moved her chair closer to the window to make the most of the waning winter light. Her pretty profile exuded an almost tragic sadness. No doubt she was mulling over their earlier conversation and struggling with what to do about Callum. Minded of how she'd once fought her feelings for Ewan, Brianna was hard-pressed not to rise from bed and give her friend a consoling hug.

Alys jabbed the bodkin into the collar of the christening robe she was stitching for Brianna's bairn. She'd begged Brianna to let her take over the task, and Brianna had consented, hoping it might distract her friend from her sorrows for a few hours at least.

"By Saint Simeon's bones, look what I've done!" Alys pulled away, sucking at her finger.

Brianna had never known Alys to drop a stitch. Nor had she ever before heard her friend curse.

She set the hoop aside and started up. "I must get some water to wash this out, otherwise it will stain."

"Leave it."

"But—"

"Nay buts." Brianna gentled her tone. "It is a baby gown, Alys. I expect it will accumulate a great many stains before my son or daughter has done with wearing it."

Alys sat back down. Brianna made a show of returning her book but she could not concentrate and for once, the baby's kicking was not to blame.

Thinking back to Chaucer's pardoner, she asked, "Alys, where were you and Alexander wed? You never did say."

Alys lifted her head. Though her pretty visage showed no sign of reproach, she must be wondering why Brianna brought up such a sore subject. "We wed in Portree. He bribed a priest from St. Andrew's to marry us. But even then, it wasna done proper in the church but in the inn where we stayed."

"That's rather unusual, is it not?"

Alys shrugged. "I suppose it is. Had Alasdair not been on the way, money or not I'm not certain he would have done the deed."

"Hmm." Brianna picked up her book and pretended to read.

Milread said pregnancy often sharpened the second sight in women so inclined. Ever since Brianna had felt the baby's first stirrings, her intuition had seemed especially keen. She had a ticklish feeling at the tip of her nose, a twitching that came over her these days when something didn't smell quite right. Alys's first marriage wanted looking into and the sooner the better.

7

"Brother! Faith but this is a happy surprise." Ewan crossed the chamber and clasped Callum in a hearty hug.

Still awkward with showing affection, Callum returned the embrace as best he could. Stepping back, he looked into his twin's face, a near mirror image of his own. Though Ewan was younger by mere minutes, still he would always be Callum's baby brother.

Ewan clapped him on the shoulder. "When I sent for Milread, I never expected you would come, too, though in truth I'm glad of it."

Like most of the actions Callum had taken in the course of his life, his journey to Skye was motivated by simple selfishness. He hadn't been able to bear being in his castle without Alys. Everywhere he turned, everywhere he looked, he saw her or rather the ghost of her.

"Brianna is recovered?" he asked, already knowing the happy news and yet hoping to shift the conversation away from him.

Ewan nodded. "It wasn't the bairn but the gooseberry tarts she'd eaten before bed. She has sworn off sweets and I have sworn off nagging—for now." He ended with a laugh.

Mired in his misery, still Callum couldn't help but

note that his brother looked weary and worried. Once he would have found such domesticity to be a bore, but not so now. Loving Alys truly had changed him for the better. It was also tearing him apart. Even though days had passed, the memory of watching her ride out of his castle gates still wracked him, fresh as the slashes on his palm. That she was beyond his protection was the source of almost constant anxiety.

"You must be parched from your journey." Ewan poured two goblets of wine and handed one to Callum. "Brie will want to see you shown to your chamber and a bath made ready."

Callum took the wine, grateful for something to do with his hands. These days they did little more than hang idle at his sides.

"Dinna trouble yourself on my account. I can always go to the mountain if need be. You do still keep the bathing tent there?"

Preparing a full bath in the dead of winter was a time-consuming task involving heating water enough to fill a trough and then bearing the buckets up many flights of steep stairs.

Ewan nodded. "Aye, Brie and I go ourselves sometimes to steam and…well, be private, though usually in the spring."

Callum didn't have to imagine what "being private" entailed. Bathing together was one of many intimacies married couples shared and yet another pleasure he and Alys had never had the chance to experience. Imagining how lovely she would look wet, he raised his goblet and drank deeply.

As if reading his thoughts, Ewan said, "Brianna and I were much aggrieved to hear of the sad ending to your wedding."

Thinking Milread lost no time, he dropped into a tapestry-covered chair. "Och, Ewan, you above anyone ken the life I lived before Alys. I've lain with women I couldn't begin to love, taken pleasure for my own selfish sake without thought to any other. As a youth, I tormented you without mercy. When you confessed to plighting your troth with Brianna that fair day, to giving her your flute as a token of your bond, I never tired of calling you out for the weak-minded folly of falling in love. And now…"

"And now," Ewan prompted.

Callum drew in a deep breath and braced himself. The tables were at last turned. His brother was about to have his chance to gloat, and Callum knew he had every right to do so.

"Now that I know what it means to love and be loved in return, I would fall upon my knees and beg your forgiveness."

Instead of heckling, Ewan sent him a look of sympathy. "I see you have grown a heart at last, for you wear it on your sleeve."

Callum drank more wine. "I would that I had not, for I have grown one only in time to see it crushed beneath an Outlander's heel."

"One never knows what life may bring. When I first learned Brie had wed her cousin, Donald, I believed with all my heart that she was lost to me forever. Who could have divined that in a few years she would be both widowed and my wedded wife?"

Callum nodded. "And yet you had the great good fortune to be abducted and bound to your lady's bed. If I thought I was relinquishing Alys to a better man, a man more like you, I would bear the parting with more grace. But I do not believe Alexander Field is a better man."

Along with showing himself the codless scut of Callum's earlier estimation, he was a bully. He couldn't begin to deserve Alys. He didn't deserve her. He didn't care about making her happy. It was clear to Callum he didn't mean to try. Denying her the comfort of the litter was all the proof he needed.

Ewan nodded. "I do not believe so, either."

Callum lifted his cup, and then nearly choked on the swallow he took. They'd been within Ewan and Brianna's fortress walls not yet an hour. Had Milread truly had the time to tell them so much?

Drawing the cup down, he asked, "How so?"

Ewan stared at him strangely. "Alys is here. She and Field arrived yesterday eve. I thought you must know."

Alys was there! Callum shot up from his seat. "How is she? *Where* is she?"

Ewan laid a staying hand on his shoulder. "Draw it mild, my brother. I ken your eagerness and its good reason, but before you seek her out, you need to contrive a plan. This husband of hers, this Englishman, is a cunning cur. Even without the pockmarks, I could not like his face."

Out of the corner of his eye, Callum caught sight of Brianna passing by the open doorway. She stopped in her tracks and entered.

"Callum, what a grand surprise this is, grand indeed." She beamed at him.

Advanced pregnancy must have altered her indeed. They'd put their differences behind them before she'd married his brother, still he'd never known her to greet him with quite such enthusiasm.

"Merry Christmas, Brianna." He turned to her and bussed her cheek. Stepping back, he surveyed her, heavily pregnant but radiant, clearly in the bloom of health. "You look well, my lady. I am glad to see you so."

Ewan crossed to his wife's side. "And I mean to keep her so." Laying a hand on her elbow, he guided her over to a brocade-covered chair with all the care one might employ in the handling of rare porcelain. The display of conjugal tenderness tore at Callum's heart. He had treated Alys in such a gentle and loving manner and would have continued to do so for all their days. Now owing to Alexander Field, he would never have that chance.

He waited until she was seated and then came directly to the point. "I know Alys is here."

She nodded. "Aye, sweet creature, she insisted on coming to tend me. I last left her sewing in my solar. She is as yet unaware you are here." Brianna hesitated. She cleared her throat. "I am given to think that not all is as it should be with her marriage."

"Why is that?"

"I have never before heard of a Christian marriage conducted in an inn, but according to Alys, the priest who joined them did so not at a church's altar rail but at a taproom's groaning board. Do you not find that odd?" Her cool green eyes awaited his answer.

Callum nodded. "Aye, I do."

He harkened back to his proposal when she'd

confided as much. The shady circumstance of her first marriage was obviously a source of shame, though he'd not given much thought to it before now. From there his thoughts flew to Field's Christmas Day boast.

The parish records will bear me out...

Ere now, Callum had never thought to question the validity of Alys's prior marriage. Like everyone else, he had accepted it as fact. But this latest bit of news cast a shadow over that surety. Annulments weren't all that common but they weren't unheard of, either. Could it be that he and Alys might have a future together after all?

"I will leave for Portree at first light and examine these documents for myself." He raked a hand through his hair and admitted, "Faith, I am almost afraid to hope again."

Brianna sent him a sympathetic look. "But you must, we all must. Just as the sky always appears darkest before the dawn and the danger at its most dire before the rescue, so do troubles such as yours appear at their most hopeless just before the solution is hit upon. If our two clans can come together after almost a generation of distrust and antipathy, if your brother and I can come together and love again after a decade of deception and feuding and aye, death, do you still discount the possibility that this matter of you and Alys may yet be mended?"

Callum shook his head, feeling dark doubt trickle back in. "When we parted, she admitted to having feelings for Field. If he truly makes her happy, I...I would not want to stand in the way of that."

Brianna bit her lip. "Before you leave for Portree, seek out Alys. I willna say more, only that you must speak with her or better yet, listen to what she has to say."

He nodded. "Aye, I will go to her now. Not all the hounds of Hell or one Outlander cur will keep me from her." He rose and strode to the door.

On the threshold, he hesitated. No matter how hard he rode, the trip to Portree and back would take two days. By then, Alys might well be on her way to England. Once she and Field crossed the border, she could be gone for good.

He wasn't accustomed to humbling himself. He wasn't accustomed to asking for help. In truth, he was hard pressed to recall a single time when he'd asked for aid from another human being. But standing on the threshold he realized he couldn't save Alys all on his own.

Dividing his gaze between Brianna and Ewan, he swallowed the last of his pride and admitted, "I need your help."

Hands resting atop his wife's shoulders, Ewan shook his head. "You are my brother, my twin. We've shared not only the same blood but our mother's womb. Whatever help I can render, know that it is yours."

Brianna nodded. "When our clans united, we became a family. We are your family, Callum. Whatever aid we may render you, we will render it freely and gladly."

Deeply moved, Callum said, "I cannot think Field will want to bide here long, certainly not once he learns I am here, as well. I need you to find some means of detaining him until I return."

Brie broke into a broad and rather wicked smile. "It is good that you brought Milread back to us, Callum. I suspect she will be more than willing to concoct a very special Christmas caudle for our dear Master Field."

AFTER EIGHT HOURS IN THE SADDLE, Father Fearghas
was more than happy to stop at an inn for the night. The
run at a breakneck pace from the parsonage to his
tethered mule had sapped him. Even as a young man,
he'd never been especially spry. He badly needed to
refresh his corporal self with food and drink and rest.

He stepped inside to the promising aroma of roasting
meat. The innkeeper stepped out from what must be the
kitchen, wiping her hands on her apron.

"Good Eve, Father. How can I help you? Are you lost?"

"Not lost, good wife, but in sore need of bed and
board for the night."

One thick eyebrow lifted. "At Christmastide?"

Father Fearghas felt a niggling of annoyance. "The
reason for my journeying is no concern of yours, my
good woman. Suffice it to say 'tis in the service of the
Lord. You'll find my needs simple and my wants few.
Whatever you have on the spit will serve me nicely."

Scowling, she shook her kerchief-covered head.
"That meat is for my family's Yuletide feast. I have
seven mouths to feed and but one meager goose."

Father Fearghas heaved a sigh, calling upon the Lord
to grant him patience yet again. "In that case, whatever
you have in the stewpot will serve me nicely."

Again, she shook her head. "Scraped clean."

Pitching his voice higher, he said, "Och, woman,
what have you to serve me?"

"Oysters."

"Oysters? *Only* oysters?"

She nodded.

Fearghas hesitated. Shellfish could be a dodgy thing

and oysters gave an especially bad report. Moreover, oysters were said to be the food of love, increasing the sexual appetite, yet another reason a man of the cloth might abstain.

She folded her arms across her breasts. "Aye, 'tis Christmastide, though twelve days of cooking scarce makes it a holy day for me. I've enough work to feed my own folk without cooking for an empty inn. Oysters, 'tis what I have, *all* I have, so you can take 'em or leave 'em."

Father Fearghas paused to ponder. Not a morsel had passed his lips since he'd broken his fast that morning and he'd raced from the parsonage to his mule like a veritable Hermes. The growl from his stomach was the settling of it.

"Very well, oysters it is."

She gave a mollified grunt and led him into the empty taproom where she seated him by the banked peat fire.

Needing something to knock the chill from both his bones and the room he asked, "Have you any wine? If not a respectable ale will do."

She snorted. "Nay wine and as for ale, keg's gone dry. Whiskey, 'tis all I've got. Take it or—"

"I know, I know, take it or leave it. I'll take it."

She brought the whiskey, slamming the flagon upon the unclothed table. Being the Almighty's messenger was thirsty work. Ordinarily he took no strong spirits, sticking to ale and well-watered wine, but since whiskey was all the drink to be had, what choice had he?

By the time she returned, Father Fearghas was on his second cup of whiskey and feeling far warmer and merrier indeed. She set the trencher before him, a dozen oysters glistening raw in their pearlescent shells.

He hadn't considered they'd come uncooked. He cast a dubious look downward. "Are you certain they're fresh?"

Fisted hands resting on her ample hips, she regarded him with hard eyes. "My husband bought them from the boat just this morning. But if you dinna want them, nay worries…" She made as if to take back the plate.

Famished, Fearghas reached for the trencher with both hands, holding it firmly in place. As a man of God, he might fast at any time. But it would be beyond selfish to put his own fleshly mortification above the mission upon which the Lord had set him. Like the manna rained down upon Moses and the Israelites, God was sending him the sustenance to soldier on.

Tucking in, he allowed he was even hungrier than he'd thought. He polished off the last of the oysters, lapping up the salty brine, and called for another platter. After washing those down with the rest of the whiskey, he was a satisfied man.

Sometime later, he wove his way up the stairs to his chamber. Halfway up, his bloated belly began to bellow, great gurgling growls. Not hunger pains this time but a pain of an entirely different, entirely urgent nature.

Flinging open the door, Fearghas raced for the chamber pot as the first spasm broke.

CALLUM MET UP with Alys by chance on the turret stairs leading from the laird's solar, he heading up and she down. Saucer-wide blue eyes registered her surprise. She reeled back, and he threw out an arm to catch her.

Having his lady once more in his arms proved to be powerfully primal. He didn't stop to consider the consequences. He didn't stop to consider much of anything at all. He did what he did best, what he'd always done best. He acted.

Callum pulled her into his arms. Holding her thus, he opened the nearest doorway and hauled them both inside. To his great good fortune it led to neither a privy nor a wardrobe closet but an unfurnished chamber that appeared to be used for storage.

Shoving them behind one cloth-covered suit of armor, he said, "I must speak with you." He didn't drop his hands for fear she'd flee.

His worry on that score proved unfounded. Far from fleeing, she reached up and smoothed back the hank of hair that was forever falling into his eyes. "I thought never to see you alone again. I never thought to see you at all. Faith, my lord, you are a sight for sore eyes."

He rested his forehead against hers and breathed deeply of her springtime scent. "As are you, lady." Shaping her with his hands, it seemed as though she had lost a stone since last he'd held her. "Field, he has not…hurt you?" He stopped himself from asking more, loath to embarrass or offend her and fearful of what her answer might be.

"Nay, he hasna touched me. I asked him to grant me time and so far he has." She buried her head against him and sighed. "But how came you here, my lord?"

He couldn't credit why Field wouldn't have lain with her. She was his wedded wife, at least so far as the world knew. Whatever the reason, Callum was grateful almost beyond bearing. Assuming Milread did her work well, the Outlander would not be in any position to claim his conjugal rights for the next several days.

"I brought Milread." He stopped himself from saying just how his good deed might soon be rewarded.

Looking up at him, she admitted, "I prayed you would come. Oh, I started out praying to the Blessed Virgin for guidance on how to accept my lot and be a dutiful wife but in the end I prayed to see you again if only to tell you all those things that before I dared not."

Minded of Brianna's counsel to listen, he prompted, "What things, dearling?"

She lifted shadow-rimmed eyes to his. "When I last left you, I said I loved Alex. Only that was a lie. I don't."

Mouth dry, he searched her face, daring to hope, daring to believe. "You don't?"

She shook her head. "I love you and only you. I love you with all of my mind and all my heart and aye, all my body. I love the verra bones of you, Callum Fraser."

He'd thought as much. Still, hearing those affirming words from her sweet, lovely lips had his heart blooming like a rose in his breast. He hugged her hard. "I love you, too, Alys. I love you more than I did even a week ago when I thought you to be mine and not another man's. I want you more than I did a week ago. I'll do whatever it takes to have you, give up whatever hope of celestial salvation I may yet have for the chance to be with you."

She shook her head. "I made a vow, milord. We must content ourselves with kisses, only kisses."

"Then kisses it shall be."

Callum could wait no longer. The craving that had built inside him for the past week now threatened to combust. Backing them up against the wall, he kissed her high forehead, her closed eyelids, and the corners of her pretty rosebud mouth. He kissed her shell-shaped ears and long white neck, dallying in her throat's well. He kissed her full on the mouth, softly and gently, deeply and fully, knowing these kisses must yet be called upon to last the rest of his miserably lonely life.

Moving down the length of her, he rediscovered the landscape of her body not only with his hands but also his mouth. Through the layers of kirtle and underskirt and shift he kissed her small, perfect breasts, her flat belly, and lastly the apex of her thighs. The musk of her arousal filtered through the layers of wool, making his mouth water and his cock throb. He kissed her because he couldn't get enough of kissing her, because he never wanted to stop kissing her, because nay matter what he found or didn't find in Portree, she was his lady, his Christmas bride, and always would be.

He straightened, chafing his beard-roughened cheek over hers like a brand. "Not until the day when you're mine entire will I rest content or otherwise."

Alys looked up at him. Her eyes were heavy-lidded and limpid, her mouth softly parted and moist. "I would make you content for a little while at least." She slid to her knees at his feet.

Shocked, Callum reached down to pull her up. "It is I who should serve you, lady."

But Alys would have none of it. She shook her head, an almost wild look upon her. "After today we will never be alone like this again. We *must* never be alone like this again. But for now, these few precious moments, I would taste of bliss." She reached beneath his kilt and slid her hand up his thigh.

Watching her, Callum wondered if he might be dreaming. The beauty of her kneeling there, her hair and clothes in delicious disarray, her rosebud mouth moist and swollen and pink, rendered him mute.

Lifting his plaid, she nuzzled him with her cheek. He felt the sigh she breathed in his very bones.

She looked up at him with a small smile. "You promised me twelve nights of twelve verra different pleasures. I would give you one at the least."

She took him in her hand, not tentatively, but firmly. Feeling the surety of that slender-fingered touch, Callum feared he would shatter into a million shiny shards.

"Alys, nay—"

"Just kisses, my lord, only kisses." She angled her face and guided him to her mouth.

8

Alys had never before given thought of a man's member being beautiful but Callum's was very much so. She ran her hand along the length of him, savoring his smoothness, testing his weight. Long and thick and perfectly formed, he pulsed against her palm in sync with her own sex's steady strumming.

Lowering her head, she lapped at the glistening cockhead, savoring his scent, his brine. It had been years since she'd taken a man in her mouth. Ere now, she'd never greatly cared for the act. But this was Callum, her love and her lord, and she couldn't wait to have him inside her in this, the one way she still might.

"Just kisses, only kisses." She drew him into her mouth.

The stone floor was hard and cold beneath her knees, Callum hard and warm inside her mouth. Nibbling, nuzzling, suckling, she pleasured him with lips and tongue and teeth. With every stroke, she contrived to drive him that much nearer to madness.

He shuddered against her. His hand descended upon her shoulder. "My sweet lady, you must cease now. You must. I—"

But Alys was in no humor to be denied. She anchored

her hands to his hips and held fast. She wanted Callum, she wanted all of him. She wanted him inside her, she wanted him to come inside her, and if she wasn't ready to dare damnation, she would at least grant them both a lesser sin. A few sweeps more of her tongue had his inner thighs trembling, his hips bucking toward her, his knees ever so slightly buckling. And then…

He snapped back his head and cried out, "Alys…my lady!"

His release struck like a summertime storm, sudden, intense and violent. Lesser tremors followed suit, ripples of thunder after the cloudburst. Holding fast to his firm buttocks, she pulled him against her, inside of her, milking the warm, rich cream of him, refusing to take less than all he had to give.

His body finally gave way. Feeling the tension in his muscles slacken, she sat back on her heels and smiled. "Are you content now, my lord?"

He reached down and lifted her up. Pushing her hair back from her damp forehead, he speared her with stark eyes. "Ere now I'd nay notion torment could be so bittersweet, that Hell could hold so verra much of Heaven." He left her, then took one of the dust sheets and spread it upon the floor. "My lady?" He held out his hand.

She took it and joined him, settling herself against him on the ground. Lying with her head pillowed upon his shoulder, she felt an unaccustomed contentment roll through her. She wasn't entirely sure but she thought they might have slept, for a minute or an hour she could not know. When she opened her eyes again, he lay on his side facing her, the strained look for now gone from his features. Like a miser hoarding gold, Alys sought to gather and store every detail of him—the beauty of his broad chest revealed by the open shirt, the musky mingled scents of sweat and arousal and evergreen, the silken texture of his mussed hair when she reached up and brushed the unruly lock back from his brow. The angry *A* scarring his hand, the wound finally beginning to scab.

She sighed. Callum Fraser would always be laird of her heart, love of her life. He was as much a part of her as any limb or organ. And yet circumstances being what they were, they each had to find a way to move on, do their duty, and learn to live without the other. They must never be alone like this again. Once they rose from this room, they must part as friends and be lovers no more. Before they did, there was nothing she wanted left unsaid between them, nothing undone she wanted to later regret.

She pressed a kiss to his proud forehead. "I love you, my lord."

His eyelids fluttered open. He looked over at her and smiled. "I ken you do and yet 'tis glad I am to hear you say it, for now that I've grown a heart, I'd be loath to be left alone in this loving matter."

"You are most certainly not alone." Tracing circles in the hair on his chest, she admitted, "Last night I lay abed thinking of you. I hoped my thoughts might carry me into dreaming but I lay awake a long time imagining us together like this. Now I have this beautiful memory to last me a lifetime." She hadn't wanted to spoil their short time with tears and yet she couldn't help choking back a sob.

He reached across and lifted her hand from his chest. Carrying it to his lips, he said, "Don't despair, lady. All may not yet be lost."

She raised her head from his shoulder. How swift she was to seize upon even the tiniest kernel of hope. "What mean you?"

He hesitated. "I leave for Portree at first light."

Portree was a pleasant enough place, with a harbor fringed by cliffs and the city itself boasting more shops and taverns and people than Alys once would have been able to stretch her mind to imagine. She'd been first married there. And yet the name brought back shameful memories of strolling along the docks in her bold yellow gown, slipping inside rubbish-strewn alleyways, saying things she didn't mean and welcoming embraces she didn't want.

Mouth dry as dust, she asked, "Why do you go there?"

He released a heavy breath. "I swore to myself I would neither give you false hope nor make you false promises, and so I will say no more until such time as I may have glad tidings to report."

Sadness settled over her. Even though she'd known this must be goodbye, she hadn't expected them to have to part so soon.

He tipped up her chin. "I will return in two days' time. In the meantime, bide you here."

She sighed and wrapped her hand about his wrist. "Alexander is eager for us to resume our journey. I do not think I can persuade him to wait out the Christmas holy days."

He sat up, bringing her with him. His expression was

somber, but still he didn't seem as distressed as she would have thought. "Plead illness if you must, only promise me you'll await my return. Whilst you are here, Ewan and Brianna can protect you."

She nodded. "I will do my best."

The happy moment spoiled, they rose to right their clothes. By mutual consent, Callum would be the first of them to venture forth first. She followed him to the closed door.

He touched her cheek. "Faith, my lady, the look upon your face slashes at my heart. I would see a smile bloom on these rosebud lips before I leave you. The gift of your smile, Alys. Can you not grant me such a small Yuletide boon before we part?" He traced her mouth, gliding his thumb along the curve of her lower lip.

She tilted her head and pressed her lips to his hurt hand. "Were I yours, I would do little else but smile."

Minded of Brianna's counsel to him the day before, he said, "Just as the sky always appears darkest before dawn and the danger at its most dire before the rescue, so do troubles such as ours appear at their most hopeless just before the solution is hit upon. But hope we must." He brushed his mouth over hers. "I will see you in the great hall below. Wait some time before coming down so that we do not seem to enter together."

She nodded, a lump in her throat. "I will."

She fell back from the door so that he might open it. Before he did, he turned back to her. "This leave-taking is our goodbye, my dearling, but not our farewell." He stepped out into the torch-lit hallway.

Watching him go, she managed a watery smile. Not

farewell, not yet anyway. She'd girded herself to bid him
goodbye and yet again that goodbye had been postponed.
Was Fate toying with them or might Milread's gods be
smiling on them at last? Until he returned she would
keep her promise and hold on to what hope she might.

CALLUM OPENED THE DOOR and peered out. Torches had
been lit. It must be later than he'd considered. He
stepped out onto the landing. Quietly and quickly he
drew the door closed behind him. For himself, he
couldn't care for the consequences, but for Alys he
cared greatly. Church law granted a man almost
complete dominion over his wife. An unfaithful wife
was considered as good as damned, fleshly mortification her only means to salvation. He hadn't forgotten
Alexander's veiled comment about the adulteress he'd
supposedly seen stoned. The penalty for whoring in
many parishes was harsh indeed, if not death then facial
branding. Callum could not be certain it would be in his
power to save her. That she might be called to suffer for
their love sent fear firing through him.

He slipped down the stone stairs as softly as he
might, willing his boots to soundlessness and wincing
at the ringing they struck. Raucous noise from the great
hall greeted him from below, signaling that the Christmastide feasting was underway. With luck, Alys was not
yet missed.

Light lapped at the curved stone walls. He found
himself facing a tapestry depicting the MacLeod clan
crest, a brace of bull's horns and motto, "Hold Fast."
Other than the time he'd seen the seal on Brianna's

letter informing him she'd abducted Ewan, he'd never given much thought to the words. Even then, he had not. He did now. For the next few days at least, he resolved to adopt that motto as his own.

He would hold fast to courage.

He would hold fast to hope.

And come what may, he would hold fast to Alys.

SEATED BESIDE ALYS at the head table in the great hall, Alex watched the byplay between The Fraser and Alys. The man had been in the castle but a few hours and yet Alex would swear he'd already found the time and means to rut with his bride. Alys had been late coming down to sup. She'd slipped into the vacant place beside him, and Alex hadn't missed the flush to her skin or the fear in her eyes. She all but reeked of sex.

He was annoyed but not really jealous. Now that the smallpox had stolen his virility, she was nothing more to him than a means to put his cherished plan into play. It was the boy, Alasdair, who was everything to him. The English lord who'd sired Alex, the same lord in whose army he'd served, was old now with no legitimate offspring. Unfortunately bastardy was a stain that could not be easily wiped away and everyone knew Alex to be the son of the cook. Two years ago, the lord and Alex had struck a bargain. Alex would bring him his firstborn son, and the lord would pass off the lad as his legitimate heir. In that way, Alex would claim his "inheritance," albeit on behalf of his child.

It was a perfect plan or so it should have been.

Alex had thought of Alys back in Portree, but the trip north was arduous. Despite his promise, he hadn't been at all certain when or if he would see her again. Nor did it matter. He was young, he was handsome, and there were English women aplenty on whom he might beget another babe.

A few days back in England, he'd fallen ill of the smallpox. His good looks were forever fouled but his body recovered its strength, or so it seemed. Only he couldn't keep a cockstand. The first few times he'd failed, he'd told himself his impotence must be a temporary state. He was weak still. He'd tried too soon. He was putting himself under excessive pressure. Given time, he would recover his virility. He hadn't. And suddenly the child he'd left behind in Alys's belly took on a sudden, priceless significance.

From the table's head, Brianna broke in upon his musing. "Master Field, will you take a cup of this most excellent mulled wine? It is Milread's special Yuletide concoction. She is verra proud of it and rightly so." She held up the chalice.

He shrugged, annoyed at the interruption. On the morrow he would leave this accursed keep if he had to drag Alys out by her hair. "I have wine yet in my cup."

Ewan frowned. "But 'tis a seasonal wine. We only make it for the Christmas holy day." Leaning in, he whispered confidentially, "For God's sake, man, drink it down. You know how emotional women can be, breeding ones especially." He lifted the cup to his own lips, swallowed and swiped his hand across his mouth.

Alex chuckled to himself. So the Fraser's twin was henpecked. Were Brianna MacLeod his woman, she'd dance a far different tune.

Still, before he and Alys set out again, he'd hopes of trading in his tired nag for one of Brianna's excellent Highland horses. There was no harm in courting some Christmas goodwill.

"Verra well, I'll try it."

Ewan passed him the cup. For the first time since he'd arrived with Alys, the lady laird smiled at him.

"You have never tasted wine quite like this, I assure you," she boasted, her green-eyed gaze fixing on his face.

Wondering what all the fuss was for, Alex took it. Berries floated atop a sea of rich ruby. He took a swallow, finding the taste passably pleasant if oversweet. He started to pass the remains to Alys, but Ewan caught his wrist.

"'Tis a man's drink. Women are nay permitted to partake. It gives them all manner of unnatural notions, if you ken my meaning." He punctuated the explanation with a wink.

Alex did. A man's drink, he liked the sound of that. He set the rim between his lips and tossed the remainder back.

LATER THAT NIGHT, Ewan left the great hall where the Christmastide merrymaking was still underway and headed for the solar he shared with Brianna. Grateful that their plan to dose Field had gone off so smoothly, he stepped inside their chamber. Brie lay propped up in their bed, their cherished copy of Chaucer's *Canterbury Tales* resting open on her mounded belly. Judging by the faraway look in her straightaway gaze, she had not turned a page in some time.

He crossed the room to the bed. He knew his lady well. Hers was not a happy face.

"Faith, you had me frightened when you seemed to take a sip from that cup."

Coming to stand beside her, he reached down to stroke her lovely loosened hair back from her forehead, most definitely furrowed in a frown. "Sleight of hand is but one of my many talents. The purgative never so much as touched my lips."

She let out a relieved breath. "I thought as much and yet still…"

"I comprehend you completely." He laid a stroking hand on her belly, thinking this mutual loving was at times a bramble-riddled road. "When your cramping commenced, you fair near took ten years off my life. If aught were to befall you…"

She cut him off with a look. "You worry yourself unduly, my love. Women have been birthing babies since Eve." She glanced down at her stomach and covered his hand with her own. "God be willing, this wee one is but the first of many to come. Milread says I have the hips for breeding."

Despite his worry, he smiled. "Aye, lovely hips you have as well as the skill of using them."

The baby making was the easy part. It was the waiting and worrying afterward that was fair near killing him. Ever since she'd told him she was pregnant, he'd been equal parts delighted and terrified. When her pains had started so far from her time and with Milread still away, he'd come closer than he ever had to madness. My God, if he were ever to lose her…

The latter brought his thoughts back to his brother. Poor Callum. Ewan had never expected to be in the position of feeling sorry for his sibling, but he most assuredly did. From his own experience, he knew that to be separated from the love of one's life was a weighty burden to bear.

Mindful of his abundant good fortune, he took his seat beside his wife on the bed, the great four-poster to which less than a year ago he'd found himself chained, a hostage bound to please her and seed her with a son. How very long ago that tumultuous time seemed.

Brianna sighed. "I am thinking of Callum and Alys. I cannot help it. If ever a maid deserved happiness, it is Alys. And your brother, if I had not seen him with mine own eyes, I would not have believed it. When he arrived, he seemed almost a broken man."

"Aye, I thought so, too."

"I only hope the journey to Portree brings good news." Her frown deepened. "Oh, Ewan, what if I am sending him off on a fool's errand?"

"You have given them hope and thanks to Milread's special Yuletide wine, you have bought Callum the time he needs. You can do nay more."

The corners of her beautiful mouth turned up ever so slightly. "Given how ill I felt after gorging myself on those gooseberry tarts, I can almost feel sorry for Master Field—almost but not quite."

"Milread assured me there was enough purgative in that cup to keep him within arm's reach of the chamber pot for the next few days." He smoothed back the red-gold hair from her brow again, determined to soothe. "The hour grows late. 'Tis time for you, my verra pregnant lady wife, to lie down to sleep."

She pulled a face. "All I do these days is sleep and for once I'm not the tiniest bit tired." She fastened her green gaze upon his face and laid her hand on the inside of his thigh. "I can think of other ways for you to divert me."

Such bittersweet torture would make a saint of him surely. Feeling himself thickening, he gently moved her hand away. "Brie, we canna. The baby."

She smiled up at him, putting him in mind of a marmalade-colored cat coveting a dish of rich cream. "Oh, but we can. Milread assures me that coupling, provided 'tis done gently, is good for pregnancy pains."

Ewan hesitated. He reached for her hand and put it back only lower. "I wouldna wish to act against a midwife's counsel."

Her clever hand commenced stroking. "I thought as much."

Gently, very gently he moved to straddle her. With a sigh, Brianna slid down on her back beneath him. Her flame-colored tresses poured over the pillows. Bracing a hand on either side of her, he leaned down to brush his lips across hers.

Pulling back, he looked deeply into her beautiful, beloved face. "I love you, Brianna of the MacLeods. And I am bound to you, my lady, bound not only to please but also to love and honor you for the rest of our days. Only now the chain leads not from these bedposts but from the chambers of my heart."

SITTING ON THE STOOL brushing out her hair, Alys watched Alex walk toward her in the mirror. He hadn't approached her sexually since that first night, for which she was profoundly grateful. Other than when he rose in the mornings to relieve himself, she never saw him naked. She heartily hoped to keep it that way.

Drawing up behind her, he settled his hands upon her shoulders, a habit of his she was coming to hate. "You were late coming down to sup. Your erstwhile bridegroom looked as though he must be missing you. Once you finally deigned to join us, he couldn't take his eyes from you."

She swept her hair to the side and kept on brushing, hoping to hide how her hands shook. "You imagine things."

"Do I?" His fingers curled about her shoulders like cuffs. "Where were you?"

Even though she'd anticipated the question, fear settled into the pit of her stomach. "I had a task to do for Brianna. She does not get about so well these days."

His breath beat down upon the back of her neck. "She has a household of servants, does she not? Could she not send one of them?"

She wetted her dry lips. "It was of a…personal nature."

"She will have to learn to do without you soon enough."

She stalled in midstroke. "What do you mean?"

Shrugging, he stepped back. "I weary of this place. The same feast-day fare, the same dull mummers and Ewan departing the company in the early hours to make haste to his big-bellied sow of a wife… It grows tedious. I would be on our way. We will leave in the morning after we break our fast."

Heart pounding, she set the brush down and turned to face him. "Brianna has asked me to stay on for the birth. 'Tis only another six weeks. By then it will be spring and the traveling made easier."

He scowled. "I cannot lollygag about like some lackey waiting for the bitch to whelp."

Alys resisted the urge to use the brush's chased silver backing to beat him about the head. "Brianna is my verra dear friend. Beyond that, we are indebted to her."

"How so?" His patchy eyebrows rose to meet the scars on his scalp line.

She set the brush down and pivoted on the bench toward him. She'd told him the tale twice now and still he couldn't bother to remember. He really was the very worst of fathers. "Were it not for her, Alasdair would be in the hands of the burgher's widow, lost to me—to us."

"Right, that." Crouching, he braced a hand on either side of the dressing table, trapping her between his arms. He leaned down, shoving his face close to hers, so close she could smell the wine on his breath. "Tell me, wife. Does this desire of yours to dally have aught to do with a certain lovestruck laird's arrival, hmm?"

Feeling like a beast caught in a hunter's snare, she pressed her lips together and steeled herself not to show her fear.

"It will be good for you to get away from here. Those nights when we met in your father's barn, you could scarcely wait until I bolted the door to open your legs for me." He slid one hand down the front of her, settling it atop her sex. "I still remember how sweet you ran when we rutted. Such zeal must have served you well on the docks of Portree."

Alys froze. The only thing she was sensible of was

her heart, which felt as though it might break through her chest at any time. "What did you say?"

He hesitated, some of the color draining from his scarred face. "Aye, I know of your past. You made quite a name for yourself amongst the sailors."

He hooked his hands under her arms and hauled her to her feet. His penis brushed her belly. She steeled herself for him to hurt her, but he felt flaccid as a jellied eel.

Her shock must have shown on her face for he dug hard fingers into her arms. "What was your price, Alys? How many ducats for the act? Did you cost cheap or dear?"

"Given that you deserted me and your unborn child and then let me think you dead, I wonder that you care." She hadn't owned how angry she was ere now.

"Nay matter. We will leave Scotland and the scene of your shame soon enough."

Minded of her promise to Callum, she dug in her heels. "I willna. 'Tis Christmas, the first Christmas our son is old enough to ken. Alasdair will have his holy day among those who love him."

His face contorted. "You are my wife. You will do as I say!" He hauled back his arm and hit her.

The open-handed blow sent her sprawling. The bench broke what otherwise would have been a bad fall. She lifted her swimming head to look at him. The mottled skin and twisted lip were nothing to her now. It was his twisted soul and evil eyes she couldn't abide.

Pressing a hand to her stinging cheek, she didn't flinch. She didn't flee. Instead she stepped forward, putting herself close up to that furious, fouled face. "Strike me you may, but bully me you willna."

He dropped his hand and drew back. Heart pounding, she stepped past him and walked over to the urn of washing water. Leaning down, she splashed cool water on her cheek. Given the sting, there would be swelling and possibly a bruise on the morrow. It was fortunate Callum would be gone. Were he to see her so, she might well find herself a widow after all.

She blotted her cheek dry, straightened, and turned to face him. "If you feel such contempt for me, I wonder you didna stay away." Married or not, how she wished he had.

"I didn't come for you, you stupid slut. I came for my son."

There, he'd said it. She'd suspected as much. Hearing it was almost a relief.

Crying from the crib sent her rushing across the room. She lifted Alasdair into her arms. "Hush, dearling, Mother's here."

From across the chamber, Alex watched them with smoldering eyes. "You coddle him."

"And if I do? I am his mother."

Wailing, Alasdair beat his tiny fists against her. "Kitty. Want kitty."

Alys sighed. She rubbed slow circles along the baby's back, seeking to soothe him. "Cat lives with Milread now. She is taking verra good care of him for us. Now close your eyes so the faeries can come and sprinkle you with their special sleepy-time dust."

Alex blew out a breath. "The brat's bawling is

enough to make my ears bleed. If he doesn't close his clapper, he can sleep in Milread's chamber, too."

Alys opened her mouth to say that he was welcome to make his bed elsewhere but glancing down she saw that Alasdair had fallen asleep against her shoulder. Relieved, she put him back down and drew the small coverlet atop him.

She rested her forearms on the crib rail, her heart fisting with all the love she felt for this tiny, perfect being. "There, there, my little lordling, nay worries, for Mother's here to banish the boogie men." She reached down and stroked his hand with her finger, tears filling her eyes. "God be willing, Mother will always be here to comfort you."

"God be willing, indeed." Alex crossed the chamber toward them.

Alys snapped upright. Feeling like a lioness guarding her cub, she stepped between him and the crib.

His cold gaze raked over her. "He will grow up and wish to be free of your clinging soon enough. Still, were I you, I'd take pains to please me lest I take him with me to England and leave you behind."

Cold fear ripped through Alys and with it a savage protectiveness. "Only a monster would separate a child from his mother." Not since the burgher's widow had stolen Alasdair had she come so very close to wishing someone dead.

He lifted his lip, making the crook more pronounced. "Obey me and there will be no need." He moved closer. "Now come here, wife, and give us a kiss. I would have us be friends again."

She moved to shove him but before she could, he doubled over. Beneath the scars, his face drained. "Poisoned, I am poisoned." Clutching his belly, he backed away from her, grabbed the chamber pot and raced with it across the room to the privacy screen.

Alys walked over to the front of the screen. Judging from the sounds coming through, he was ill indeed. Like as not he'd only eaten something disagreeable to him but if he cared to credit her as a poisoner, then so be it.

"Mark me, Alex. If you ever try taking Alasdair from me or in any way keeping me from him, I will kill you. Only it willna be with poison. I will use my dirk to slit you from ear to ear, cut off your cods for my trophy and never, ever, think of you again."

THE FOLLOWING MORNING at first light Callum rode to Portree at full gallop, sparing neither his mount nor himself. Despite Ewan's assurance that Field had drunk sufficient of the "special wine" to necessitate confinement to his chamber, Callum wished to take no chances. The sooner he arrived and made his way to the church, the sooner he might return to the MacLeod Castle and Alys. He only prayed that when he did, he would do so bearing glad tidings. He'd asked her to hope again. In the bright light of morning that request bore a heavy weight of responsibility.

Tethering his lathered horse to the post, he crossed the cobbled courtyard to the church. Stepping inside the narthex, he spotted a young acolyte. To his great good fortune, the mass had just finished. A swift explanation of his purpose sweetened with a donation of ducats for the repair of the roof won him a private audience with the priest, Father Seumas.

Sitting across from Father Seumas, he asked, "Do you remember the couple of which I speak? They would have married nigh on two years ago."

The good father nodded. "Christian marriage is but one of the many rites of the church recorded in the records ledger. Ordinarily casting my mind back that far would present some difficulty, but an Englishman stands out in the memory. Aye, I mind him. Tall, blond and bonny with a soldier's swagger."

Callum nodded. That was Field all right, or at least it had been before the smallpox fouled his face and blackened his heart. "And his bride, do you remember her, as well?"

He nodded slowly. "She wasna a parishioner, either." He scrunched his forehead. "She was Scotswoman, fair-haired and from the Lowlands."

Callum's heart sank. "Do you remember aught else?"

The priest squinted as if thinking back. "I seem to recall she was a tall lady, gangling some might say."

Callum's heart lifted a notch. Alys was neither tall nor gangling.

"And she had a haughty demeanor. She made it plain my humble church wasna near good enough for her."

Callum's hopes and his heart lifted further, for his lady hadn't so much as a single haughty bone in all her petite and lovely body. "I'd like to see the parish records for myself."

"Of course." The priest called for the book. While

they waited, he said, "You are the second man this week to request to see the records book."

"There was another?"

"Aye, he is a fellow priest and the brother of our anchoress here. He never did say what he was about. Disappeared without so much as a by-your-leave. It was all verra strange."

Before he could give the subject further thought, the young priest returned with the ledger and set it down on the table between them.

Father Seumas opened it. "Now what year was it that holds your interest?"

Callum answered, "1458."

The priest turned to the requested year. Flipping through, his eyes popped and his jaw dropped. "By all the saints!"

Callum leaned across the table. It took every whit of patience he possessed to keep from snatching the book away.

"Why that's verra odd! The page is missing. Not missing but torn out."

Father Seumas turned the book so Callum could see. A page was indeed missing from the month of April, torn out and by the look of it recently so.

The missing page told Callum he must be on the right track. But to be safe, he further examined the book, going backward in time by several years. But there was no bridegroom with the name of Field listed.

The parish records will bear me out...

"There is another thing that strikes me as strange."

Callum looked up from the book. "And what is that?"

"Several months later, a letter was sent in care of me for a young Lowlands woman living in town, a pretty young lassie heavily pregnant. 'Twas verra sad, a letter on behalf of her husband back in England. He'd caught a fever or some such and died. His name was Alexander Field and though I dinna mind it at the time, he must have been the same Alexander Field whom I wed in this verra sanctuary. Only..." He stopped himself.

On tenterhooks, Callum demanded, "Only?"

"The pretty pregnant lassie who claimed to be his wife, the one for whom I read his letter aloud, wasna the bride I wed him to."

The codless bastard had been bluffing all along! There was indeed a marriage, only not to Alys. Already wed, Field must have arranged for the sham ceremony to keep her with him. Once he'd tired of the game, he'd announced the imminent need to return to his army post. Alys had admitted that when they'd first met, Alex had been exceedingly handsome with winning ways to turn a maid's head. Callum didn't doubt the rogue could be charming when the need arose. Who knew how many others he'd played the same cruel trick upon? He might have bastards scattered across the two kingdoms. Why come back for Alasdair?

He who'd never before prayed for anyone or anything had had his very first prayer answered! Alys was as good as free! Alex Field wielded no husband's rights over her. He didn't wield any rights at all. As for Alasdair, the boy belonged to Alys and no other.

After a sennight of darkest despair, the rush of relief

was heady stuff. For the first time in his life, he was drunk on hope, drunk on happiness, drunk on a future that seemed once again brimming with love and laughter and wonderful possibilities.

He'd promised Alys a Twelvetide of unforgettable nights as well as a lifetime of never ending Christmas. He would be able to make good on both promises after all.

He couldn't wait to begin celebrating.

9

Crofter's Cottage
A village a few leagues from MacLeod Castle

MORAG SAT on a backless bench before the dressing mirror meticulously tweezing errant hairs from her brow. She was enormously proud of her high forehead, which she managed to hold back a full finger's length from the line of her natural scalp.

Arms crossed to ward off further cramping, Alex asked, "Don't you find all that plucking to be painful?"

She shrugged bony shoulders. "Beauty exacts its price. And you do find me beautiful, don't you?" She turned about to face him, craning her long neck.

He didn't find her looks more than passable, not that it mattered anymore. Even though they lived apart most happily, he in London and she in Portree, she was still his wife. When he'd sent for her a few days ago, his message hinting at a mutually beneficial enterprise, she'd heeded his call.

Because he still needed her and would for a while, he dutifully answered, "Your beauty shines like a beacon, my love." He leaned over and brushed a kiss over her thin lips.

She sat back, apparently mollified for the moment. "You should have been a courtier, not a soldier." She scrutinized his face, her cool expression more curious than repulsed. "You're certain you won't have me try covering those scars? I'm clever with paint and powder. You might be surprised."

He shook his head, the prospect making his ruined flesh crawl. Once the pox pustules had turned putrid, he'd endured weeks of salving and bandaging and burning off the diseased skin before the lesions healed sufficiently to scab. The experience had left him with a fierce dislike of being touched, especially on his face.

Fortunately Morag didn't seem put off by his spoiled looks. Theirs was a marriage of like minds, a union of twisted kindred souls. Both were greedy, grasping and entirely devoted to themselves. His wife was far too transfixed by the face she saw in the mirror to care greatly for what had become of his.

"You're clear on the plan?" he asked her.

Spending the better part of the past two days between the bed and chamber pot had firmed his resolve if not his bowels. It was time, past time, to move forward with getting his son and himself back to England.

"Aye, I am." She nodded. "And afterward my reward will be?" She lifted one painted brow and waited.

Knowing her so well, he'd anticipated the question. "Once we present Alasdair to my father, you will be installed in his castle and given all due deference as his mother along with whatever riches you desire."

She lifted her heavy-lidded eyes. "Is that all?"

Alex shrugged. She was a bloodthirsty bitch, but then again that was what made her so very useful.

He hesitated, casting his thoughts back to Alys's threat just as he'd fallen ill. Cut off his cods, indeed! "You may have Alys's empty head on a platter, provided you've the heart to take it," he finished. Morag had taken the banishment from the MacLeod's great hall hard indeed.

Smiling, she turned back to her paint pots and picked up her brush. "My husband's generosity is outweighed only by his deviousness."

The griping pains hadn't disappeared altogether but still Alex managed to smile. "In this world, lady, I have found it wise to have a goodly measure of both."

SINCE SETTING OUT THAT MORNING, Father Fearghas had made passably good time. Because it was still the holy day, the main roads were deserted beyond the occasional straggler. Taking advantage of the open space, he'd pushed the donkey hard to make back the time his late start had cost him.

The oysters had been a most unfortunate affair, emptying him of his dinner and robbing him of any hope of sleep. For the better part of two days he'd divided the hours between a seemingly rocking bed and a chamber pot fast filling. By now his innards must be as clean as Adam's upon the first day of his creation.

He rode on until nature's call could no longer be denied. He dismounted, tethered the donkey to a low hanging branch and made haste to a stand of scrubby bushes. Slipping behind, he pulled up his clothes and squatted down.

"How now, what's this, a plump partridge?"

Midstream, Fearghas shot up his head, his gaze meeting with two sets of thick, hairy legs. The limbs were attached to two burly ruffians who bore down on him. He gulped hard and let his robe drop.

The second piped up, "I think it's a plump priest, brother."

Taking hold of an arm each, they hauled him to his feet.

The first man rifled with his middle. "What do you have under your cloak there, good father? I venture 'tis a bonny fat purse to match your belly."

In the end, they divested him of his cloak, riding boots, and even the wooden prayer beads hanging from his belt. Stripped down to his smock, Father Fearghas congratulated himself on concealing the folded records page within his hose.

Arms folded, one of them suggested, "Maybe we should perform a baptism and wash away the good father's sins with a dunking in yon stream!"

"Nay!" Fearghas held up a hand. The water would be cold as a witch's tit but beyond that, dunking would ruin his precious evidence. "I canna swim," he added, hoping God would forgive him the lie. "Toss me in and I'll sink like a stone. Then it will be a murder on your hands and your immortal souls damned. Only pause to think upon the fire, the brimstone, the eternity of famine and thirst!"

They looked at him and shrugged. He suspected

they'd heard his standard priestly description of Hell many a time.

Inspiration struck, *Divine* inspiration. He dropped his voice and added, "Really big, really putrid, really painful boils down...*there*." He patted the place between his legs where the records packet rested.

The thieves' eyes grew wide. Their jaws dropped. They exchanged worried looks.

The larger of the two spoke up. "Down...*there*?"

"Aye, the verra spot." Father Fearghas punctuated the statement with a knowing nod. "If that is the manner of rest you seek for your immortal souls, then by all means toss me in. Otherwise be gone lest you spend an eternity with Beelzebub's creatures!"

The pair exchanged frightened glances. They seemed to shrink before his eyes. Arms full of the purloined articles, they turned tail and ran.

Unfortunately so did his donkey. Spooked, the beast let out a shriek and bolted, moving more swiftly than Fearghas had ever before seen. Too shaken to lay chase, he fell back against a tree.

Scouring a hand over his brow, he offered up a hasty prayer of thanks for his deliverance. Ere now, he'd never fully appreciated just how exhausting serving the Divine could be. Since setting out on his journey, he'd been purged, starved, beaten and stripped. Unless he found shelter before nightfall, death by freezing could not be far off.

He stood, brushed himself off, and foraged the foliage for a fallen twig of the requisite length and sturdiness.

Finding it, he took up his makeshift staff and continued on his way to the Fraser fortress, determined to pursue his pilgrim's mission and any further sufferings it might yet bring with a glad and joyful heart.

ALYS SPENT MOST OF THE TIME Callum was away in the kitchen garden, furiously turning up turnips and other root vegetables from the frozen earth. Even in the dead of winter with the fish pond frozen over and ice blanketing the stepping stones, the little walled place with its scrubby bushes and barren beds was her sanctuary.

But there was no refuge from her thoughts. Callum was now two days gone. He should be back any time now. She prayed and feared for him in equal measure. If the news he bore was bad, she would have to say goodbye to him yet again, this time for good, and submit herself to going to England with Alex. Alex's illness, from which he was only just recovering, had kept him mostly in bed and out of her way for two days. Pale and thin, he'd risen and rode into the village a few hours ago. With luck, she would have yet another day's sweet reprieve. Now that she'd known hope again, the thought that she might yet have to live with him as his wife was almost unbearable.

Alasdair dallied in the dirt beside her. She couldn't be certain but she thought he might be pretending the piles she made were mountains. Bundled against the cold, he at least seemed to be having a grand time.

All at once, a smile suffused his cherub's face. He dropped the dirt he'd fisted and stretched out his arms. "Papa! Papa, come!"

Alys shot up her head. Callum stood in the arched gateway. His cloak and boots were dust-covered, his face drawn with lines of fatigue, and yet he'd never been more beautiful to her. Catching her eye, his face lit with a smile.

He was smiling. That must be a good sign, it must! Heart pounding, she put down her trowel and rose on wobbly legs, brushing dirt from her knees.

Toddling to his feet beside her, Alasdair tugged on her sleeve. "Papa, come."

She touched her hand to his shoulder, gently urging him forward, praying to the Blessed Virgin she could trust that smile, Callum's smile. "Aye, dearling, I see. Go and greet him."

He hurried off, chubby legs making short shrift of the stone path despite his wobbling. "Papa!" He launched himself against Callum's legs.

"There's my lad." Callum bent, grabbed hold and swung him high in the air, winning squeals of unadulterated delight.

Watching them, Alys felt her heart squeeze in on itself. Limbs weak, she walked over to join them. Their eyes met atop Alasdair's blond head.

Callum set Alasdair down and straightened. "I have a wee gift for you, laddie."

He unlaced his sporran, reached inside and pulled out a small carved object. No Christmas Wife this time but a perfectly honed wooden horse, a miniature of the great black steed Callum rode. He offered it with a smile.

"When you're bigger, I will gift you a real horse and teach you to ride." His gaze rested on hers and this time she was all but sure of good tidings.

Alys's heart lifted further. Making future plans, referring to himself as her son's "papa," surely he would not do so had he not good news to report.

Alasdair grabbed greedily. "Horsie!" He plunked down at their feet to play with his new treasure.

Callum's eyes locked upon hers. The smile he'd worn upon stepping inside the garden broadened. "Will you not welcome me home with a kiss…wife?"

Tears filled Alys's eyes. "My lord?" Before she'd been afraid to hope and now she was afraid to believe.

"The parish records didna bear out Alexander's claim after all. It seems you were falsely wed, for he was wed already to another."

"Truly?"

"Aye, most truly. She is described as tall, bony and painted. Do you ken such a person?"

Alys scoured her brain. She'd met people aplenty in Portree, most of them men. "I dinna."

He shrugged. "It doesna signify." He stroked his big rough hand along her cheek. "Tears, my lady, on such a glad occasion?"

Until he spoke, she hadn't realized she'd started crying. Minded of Milread's previous parting words, she dashed a hand across her eyes and shook her head. "The cold but stings my eyes."

"Ballocks, you're weeping. After what I've been through, those had better be happy tears."

Hearing the smile in his voice, she smiled, too. "They are, my lord, oh, they are, the most happy."

"I will do all in my power to see that you've naything but happiness from hereon." He embraced her. His breath blew into her hair. "Ah, Alys, my sweet and beautiful Christmas bride, to think that all this terrible long week of stealth and wanting and saying goodbyes, it was always my right to hold you."

Feeling his arms tighten about her, she knew she never wanted to leave this shelter again. She slid her arms about his waist, drawing him close, hugging him hard. Faith but he was warm and strong and all hers, or so it seemed.

Chin resting atop her head, he traced soothing circles upon her back. "Come with me. There is something I would show you, a place special to me since I was a boy."

She lifted her head to look up at him. "Alasdair—" She glanced down to her son playing his toy horse about their feet.

"Go on with the both of you." Milread stood in the garden gateway, tears streaming her cheeks. Caught up in Callum, Alys had not heard her approach. Clearly she'd arrived in time to hear the good news. "I'll mind the little lad 'til you return. We'll nay venture beyond the castle grounds."

Alys hesitated. Alex was gone until nightfall, and even were he not, by the looks of him that morning, he was still too peckish to do anyone any great harm.

She glanced at Callum, duty warring with the most unbearable desire to be with him. "Verra well, so long as we return ere nightfall."

He smiled. "You have my word that we shall."

Milread came toward them and took hold of Alasdair's hand. "Go on." She lifted the boy into her sticklike arms. "Glad tidings such as these want for celebrating, aye, my lord?" She shot Callum a wink.

Alys could not defeat both of them, nor did she truly

want to. Callum had promised her a Twelvetide of
sensual pleasure, and she was more than prepared to
collect her next gift.

Dismissing her misgivings, she bowed her head.
"Thank you, Milread." She turned back to Callum. "I
feel as though I must be dreaming. Good my lord, can
this truly be?"

"Aye, it can and it is, sweetheart. I will explain all on
the way. For now, know this—you are my lady, my lady
wife, mine and no other man's, and I would give you a
honeymoon to make the saints swoon."

THEY RODE AWAY from the fortress and headed into the
Cuillin Hills. Seated in the saddle in front of Callum and
wrapped up in his fur-lined cloak, Alys had never felt
so cherished and content. Ordinarily Callum's great
beast would have terrified her. But leaning back into her
husband's strength and heat, his arms and thighs locking
like steel bands about her, her loosened curls blowing
wild about her face, she'd never felt so protected yet glo-
riously free.

They rode for nigh on two hours, skirting plunging sea
cliffs and lochs as deep as mountains. At one point, Alys
lifted her head from Callum's chest and looked back at
him. "You never did say where you're taking me."

He smiled back at her. His eyes, though tired, looked
radiant bright. "If I told you, it wouldn't be a surprise."

Thinking of how Alex had barged into their wedding
feast a week ago, she answered, "I am no longer certain
I like surprises."

Even knowing he had no power over her or their son,

she couldn't entirely dismiss him. He would have to be dealt with. She suspected Callum would not let him go without some punishment. What form retribution would take, she didn't care to consider right now.

Callum cinched his arm more tightly about her. "You will like this one."

She laughed and what a good feeling it was. "You're that sure of yourself, are you, my lord?"

He kissed the top of her head and tucked it beneath his chin. Settling back, he said, "We shall see, my lady. In good time we shall see."

They crested the steep hillside. Gossamer sheets of mist shrouded them. Looking down onto the coastline from whence they'd come, bolstered by Callum's caring and his warmth, Alys felt as though she'd ascended to Heaven already.

They must be coming on to their destination, for he slowed the horse to a walk. Secreted into the hillside, a small striped pavilion came into view. Outside, a camp fire burned. Beside the fire was a goodly sized quarry of rocks.

He reined the horse in. "Ewan and I used to come here and bathe as boys."

Alys lifted her head from his shoulder. "But these are MacLeod lands. I was given to understand the rift between the MacLeods and Frasers dates back to your fathers' day."

He dismounted. "To the generation before." Wrapping his arms about her waist, he lifted her down. "When Brianna's advisor, Duncan, made me out to be a murderer, the scurrilous lie was sewn upon verra fertile ground."

Her feet touched the earth but looking up into

Callum's tired but happy face, her head still felt very much in the clouds. "And still you risked yourselves to come here?" If she lived to be as old as Milread, never would she comprehend the ways of men.

"That's what made it fun." He grinned and took her hand, leading her inside.

She followed, wondering what awaited them within. So long as it involved the two of them alone together, she was more than happy to embrace whatever he had in mind.

"My lady." He lifted the sheepskin flap and motioned for her to enter.

Alys stepped within. The scene that greeted her put her in mind of a Christmastide fairyland. Bows of yew and holly hung from the wooden beams of the make-shift ceiling, exuding their crisp evergreen scent, Callum's scent. A large marble basin took pride of place in the center. Stone steps led down to the bottom. From the water, fragrant steam rose. Floating on the surface were more rose petals than Alys had ever before beheld.

She whipped around to face him. "A bath!" Excepting holy days, she bathed herself and Alasdair from an urn of cold water carried up from the kitchen. A full bath was a rare and longed for luxury. "All this for…me?"

He ducked inside and let the tent flap fall. "Merry Christmas, my lady."

A flagon of wine and two drinking horns had been set out on one of the wood benches along with a platter of nuts and fruits and cheeses, a re-creation of the simple wedding supper of which they'd never had the chance to partake.

Two serving wenches approached. Each girl bore

two buckets heaped with heated rocks supported on a yoke borne across her shoulders.

"My lord, my lady." Encumbered, still they both bobbed curtsies.

Alys looked over at Callum and smiled. "There is no end to your co-conspirators, I see."

He didn't deny it. "Ewan and Brianna would see us happy."

Giggling, the girls unloaded their burdens and came toward him. "May I help you disrobe, my lord?" one of them asked.

Sitting down on a bench to pull off his boots and heavy woolen stockings, Callum shook his head. "Nay, attend my lady."

Expressions disappointed, they turned to Alys. Between the pair of them, they had her stripped down to her shift in no time. Callum looked on, the heat in his eyes warming her. Being undressed before him was more powerfully erotic than Alys could have imagined. Still, some modesty remained.

When they made to raise her arms so that they might pull the shift up over her head, she halted them. "I thank you for your care, but I will manage from here on."

"*We* will manage," Callum added, and the famished look on his face brought her breasts tingling to life.

The girls backed off. They picked up their buckets and poured the hot rocks into the trough. Eddies of sweet-smelling steam arose, veiling the tent in mist.

Callum stood. As if reading her mind, he said, "They will not come back for an hour. By then the water will have cooled and it will be time for us to start back."

After the past torturous week, Alys could scarcely wrap her mind around the bounty of a whole hour to be private together.

An hour to bask in warm water and moist steam and perfect peace and safety.

An hour to speak all that was in not only their minds but their hearts, as well.

An hour to make love in any way, every way, they might wish without fear or threat.

She slid her gaze over him and smiled. "You sent the lasses away and yet you are dressed. You must be warm with all those clothes on."

Not since her whoring days had she been so bold, nor had she thought to be so again. But loving Callum and knowing now that she was his and he hers freed her.

"I am." He held her eye and he started on the buttons of his moleskin jerkin. "I wish for no hands upon me save those of my beautiful wife."

Wife. What a wondrous word that suddenly seemed. It was the second time in as many hours that he'd referred to her as such. A lifetime wouldn't be enough to tire her of being so named. The sobriquet spoken from her love's lips was as powerfully erotic as the prospect of helping him undress.

"In that case, pray let me help you…husband." Heart quickening in anticipation, she rounded her bench and walked toward him, loving how his eyes tracked her every move.

She felt her breathing hitch and not because of the thick, pungent air. Heretofore she'd only ever seen glimpses of his body. The two times they'd been together before were furtive affairs. There had been no time for undressing. But this time they were husband and wife, not only in the eyes of God and the law but also their own. They were free, finally free of fear and guilt and the need to rush. Free to make love as slowly, openly and thoroughly as they wished.

She stepped behind him and reached up, sliding the vest over his powerful shoulders and off. Laying it on the bench, she circled to the front of him. His saffron shirt was next to go. Eager to see him though she was, she also had waited a long time for this moment. She unfastened the queue of buttons as slowly as she might, bringing his beautiful broad shoulders and tapered torso into gradual view.

"You are beautiful, my lord." She trailed her forefinger down the queue of dark hair beginning below his breastbone to where it disappeared beneath his kilt.

"Not as beautiful as you, but then, nay one could be that." He wetted the pad of his thumb and used it to wipe her cheek where dirt must be streaked. "You look much as you did that verra first time I laid eyes on you."

Self-conscious, she shook her head and combed her hand through the tangles in her hair. "That is because I am a mess."

His eyes were dark with desire, his smile heartrending in its tenderness. "You are all a bride should be."

She wrapped her hands about him, unfastened his weapons belt, and laid it aside. His kilt was last to go. Reaching behind him she slowly unwound his plaid. Callum's mighty chest rose and fell with each rapid, ragged breath.

The tartan slipped from her nerveless fingers, falling to the ground. Alys sucked in her breath, suddenly feeling as if she was suffocating in the thick, moist air. She had secretly wondered how far down the queue of dark hair traveled and there was no longer any doubt. Callum stood before her, Adam in all his pre-Fall glory, the perfect man in all his fleshly perfection—chest broad, belly flat and swelling penis standing out from its nest of dark hair like a mighty staff. Taking in the turgid flesh, remembering the scent of him, the texture of him, the taste of him, she felt her mouth water and her sex cream.

Stepping past her, he squatted to test the water, the sight of his beautiful back, slim hips and firm buttocks making her mouth dry. Her skin felt feverish and hyper-sensitive, her thin shift suddenly too heavy and cumbersome to bear.

He straightened and turned to her, his stark gaze striking hers. "I would give you not only your honeymoon but your wedding day, as well, my lady."

Alys met his gaze. "And I would give you yours, my lord."

He spread an arm to indicate the enclosure. "Let this bathing tent be our chapel and this pool our bridal bed."

Alys swallowed hard and nodded, feeling as though they indeed stood on sanctified ground, a sacred place. "And these stone steps our church aisle and this unadorned shift my bridal gown, for my good lord, I would come to you as a bride."

CALLUM AWAITED HER in the water. Like a selkie shedding her seal skin, she left most of her clothing on the bench and started down the stone steps. She waded into the water, her nubile form fording a path through the rose petals, her shift forming a floating train, bringing to mind fairies and mermaids and other ethereal, fanciful beings. Like them, Callum had trouble believing she was real.

She leaned back to sluice her hair, exposing the arc of lovely long neck and slender shoulders. Callum didn't move. He didn't speak. He couldn't be sure he still breathed. He'd never before seen her wet. The thin linen of her shift clung like a second skin. Slim of waist and hip and slender of limb with small, high breasts tipped in roses, she outstripped any fantasy he'd yet to fathom.

She met him in the center of the pool. She was so much smaller than he, the water reached nearly to her shoulders. The flesh of her face and throat and shoulders glowed with the luster of well-worn pearls.

She looked up at him through her water-clumped lashes. "I love you, my lord. With all my mind and all my heart and all my body I love you. I love the verra bones of you, and I am so happy to be your wife."

Callum swallowed hard, feeling his newly mended heart swell. "I love you, too, my lady. I pledge you my honor, my fidelity, my protection and aye, my love from this day forward, for all the rest of our days." Locking his gaze upon hers, he lifted her left hand, turned it over and matched it to his, the one with the scabbed *A*. "I receive you as mine, so that you become my wife and I your husband."

Expression solemn, she held his gaze and she repeated, "As I receive you as mine, so that you become my husband and I your wife."

Heart in his throat, he broke hands. Her betrothal ring rested upon his smallest finger. The ruby flashed crimson fire, a symbol of their Christmas miracle.

He slid the ring off his finger and onto hers. "I pray you accept this ring as my token and never again take it off, for with it I thee wed. This gold and silver I thee give. With my body I thee worship, for the rest of our given days."

She lifted the stone to her lips. "I never shall."

He breathed in her scent, earthy yet delicate and still distinguishable above the greenery and roses. "Flesh of my flesh…"

Beneath the water, he glided his hands over her, shaping her tiny waist and hips, sliding upward to cup her breasts. Mapping the terrain of her body with his touch, he resolved that no hollow or crevice should remain unknown or unnoticed. He moved to the core of her, to the stiff curls between her legs, his palm stroking. Alys tipped back her head and sighed. Reading her want, he took the hem of her shift and lifted it. Through the water and steam, he saw the triangle of dark gold curls and the very beginning of delectable pink nether lips. He saw himself, as well, hard as the rocks sunken at their feet and stained a deeper hue from the water's heat.

Reaching down between them, he found her with his fingers. "Sweet my lady, I canna wait to be one with you."

She shook her head. "Dinna wait. I dinna want you to wait. We've waited long enough."

He put his hands on her waist and lifted her onto him. She went without hesitation, her legs, slender but strong, locking along his hips, her hands clutching his shoulders, her breasts brushing his chest. Her shift floated atop them, a cocoon for their loving.

She arched back, her body begging. "My lord... Callum, please!"

Callum didn't wait to be asked a second time. His cockhead pulsed against her lower belly. Shifting, he sheathed himself inside her in one long, sure thrust. Had he been a poet, he doubted he could have found the words to express the wonder of entering her on this, their very first time.

Alys's eyes flashed wide. Her gasp echoed through the tent.

"You feel like a virgin." She was very small and exquisitely taut for all she'd borne a bairn. He pulled back and entered her more gently this time.

She tilted her head back and smiled, her inner flesh pulsing. "You make me feel like a virgin."

He stilled. "Do I hurt you?"

"Nay, you dinna hurt me, my love." She slid trembling, water-warmed fingers down his face. "You heal me. You make me feel wondrous young and shiny new." She rocked against him.

Callum was deeply moved and mortally aroused. He pushed inside her again, his fingers trailing the juncture between her buttocks. Alys shivered. She ground against him, her breaths coming in little pants, her nails digging into his shoulders.

For the span of minutes, reality dissolved into the slapping together of warm, wet flesh, the smell of roses and evergreen, and the firmness of Alys's lithe little body straining to meet his. The wild, urgent look in her eyes told him she was closing in on her climax. Callum reckoned he was but a few strokes from his, as well. He vowed to wait for her.

"Flesh of my flesh…" Hands braced beneath her thighs, he pressed deeply into her.

Alys threw back her head, her moaning spiraling like steam. She clutched his shoulders harder. "Oh, Callum!"

"Heart of my heart…" He twisted his hips and thrust again, entering her at an angle.

He trailed the fingers of one hand between her buttocks and reached around to her front. He wanted to touch her everywhere at once, all at once, but he most especially wanted to touch her there. "Love of my life."

Clutching his shoulders, Alys threw back her head and screamed.

THEY LAY TOGETHER atop the blankets spread upon the floor, the cooling water tickling their toes, their bodies sensitized from the steam and the loving.

Alys's shift lay across a bench to dry. Callum picked up the vial of scented oil and drizzled it on her back, following the curve of her spine.

Resting her head on her folded arms, Alys shivered, and then sighed. "You spoil me. I could become accustomed to this."

"And so you will."

He massaged in the oil, his hand dallying in the cleft between her buttocks. Giving in to a devil's dare, he leaned over and lightly bit one taut milky lobe. "Just as I thought. Like a firm apple." Pulling back, he gave her a light smack.

Alys wriggled more in pleasure, he thought, than in any desire to get away. She looked back at him over her shoulder. Her damp hair formed a halo of ringlets, framing a face that was not only relaxed but glowing.

"We have yet more Christmas nights before Twelfth Night. You must not spend all your gifts in one day."

"I will have to come up with more beyond the twelve. Once I've finished with Field, I mean to devote endless hours to finding new ways to pleasure and delight you."

She sobered. "What *will* you do about Alex?"

Callum stalled his stroking. He let out a heavy breath and admitted, "Ordinarily I would have him executed."

She hauled herself up on her elbows. "My lord, I pray you do not. He is my son's father. And he was... dear to me once."

A week before that admission would have roused him to jealousy but they'd both been through so very much since then. The past was best set to rest in the shadow land of memory, whereas a joyous lifetime of Christmases lay ahead.

He pulled her back against him, wrapping her in his arms. "Then I will spare him for your sake, as well as Alasdair's." In response to her furrowing brow, he explained, "I want no more doubt cast upon our union. After the Christmas holy day, I will convene another court, presided over by the Old Gentlemen and myself, and before all the clans folk, I will make his treachery known."

If only he might track down that rent records page! He would give an eyetooth to have it in his possession. Still, if need be, the sworn testimony of the priest at St. Andrew's, Father Seumas, would suffice. He glanced at the hourglass above them, set out to track the time. Like the dwindling sands, the steam and scent were fast fading, the outside chill finding its way within the tented walls. It was coming on time for them to leave their Christmas fairyland for the real world where hard tasks and unsavory duties awaited. Field must be dealt with. The depth of his perfidy made him a dangerous man. He couldn't be allowed to go about freely, not any longer. The trial would not take place until after the holy days, but Field would find himself a prisoner under house arrest ere nightfall. The sooner he was clapped in irons, the safer Alys and her son would be.

IT WAS COMING ON DARK when Father Fearghas finally reached the Fraser fortress. He'd never found his mount. The bandits who'd stolen his purse had taken his cloak, as well. Frozen, footsore, and no doubt nursing an ague, still he summoned a smile as he crossed the bridge and stepped up to the gatehouse. His personal trials were nothing compared to the glad tidings he bore. Because of him, Callum and the Lady Alys could wed. Come to think of it, they were already wed. Who knew but mayhap they would name a son after him. He wasn't expecting anything. It was but a thought.

For now he would seek out the Fraser, impart his good news, and then take his weary, aching body to the comfort of his bed.

"Halt, who goes there?"

One of the pair of guards hauled him up against the stone wall. The other pointed his pike at Fearghas's throat.

Dividing his gaze between them, he said, "My good

men, you are grievously mistaken. I live here. I am a re-spected priest—your laird's priest."

They ran their gazes over him and chortled, knifing one another in the ribs. "O' course you are. And I'm the King of France and he of England."

Several times they tried sending him to the beggar's gate. They laughed at his repeated demands to be taken to Callum.

"Even if we were so addled as to take you to the Fraser, he's nay here."

Fearghas felt his faith and his fortitude sinking like twin wrecked ships. "What…what did you say?"

"He set out for the MacLeod Castle days ago. He's not expected back 'til after the holy days."

10

THEY RETURNED to Castle MacLeod as night was falling. A somber-faced Brianna awaited them within. "Alasdair is missing," she announced.

Alys felt as though the slates were sinking beneath her feet.

"What do you mean missing? He is a bairn yet whose steps are unsteady. He cannot have wandered off on his own."

Callum's arm came around her. Scarcely minding it, she swung about to Milread, who'd entered. The crone wore a bandage on her head. She looked not only old, but frail.

Tears welling, Milread shook her head. "Not wandered off, wean. Taken."

Taken. The word tolled fear into Alys's heart. Feeling as if she were in the midst of a nightmare, she listened as Milread explained how earlier she'd walked Alasdair about the beach, pointing out the sea's hidden creatures when a tall woman with a plucked forehead and painted face approached them. The woman had looked passing familiar. Milread's Third Eye had begun its telltale twitching, ever a harbinger of danger. She'd taken Alasdair and started moving away when the blow struck. A fierce pain, blinding and blazing, was the last of her memory.

Callum spoke up. "Tall, plucked and painted, you say?" He sent Alys a meaningful look. "So the priest at St. Andrew's described Field's wife."

Alys nodded, feeling as though her brain was frozen. She'd been so caught up in celebrating her new happiness, it hadn't occurred to her to wonder after the fate of Alex's wife.

Milread ended her tale by wringing her hands. "When I awoke, the wee laddie was nay where to be found. Only the castlefolk have access to that bit of beach. I thought we'd be safe."

Bending awkwardly down, Brianna draped an arm about the witch's thin shoulders. "It's not your fault, Milread. Nay one blames you."

Numb, Alys nodded. This wasn't Milread's fault. It was hers. Given Callum's news, she should have considered Alex might be up to something. She should never have left her baby behind. Now her selfishness had lost her Alasdair, mayhap forever.

Callum demanded, "What is being done to find him?"

Brianna answered, "Ewan has two of our finest warriors with him to search. They have taken torches and are combing the beach and the—" she hesitated, gaze veering to Alys "—cliffs. Field, too, seems to be missing. The cupboard in your chamber has been cleared out."

Alys nodded, feeling as if she were working a tavern puzzle and yet missing a crucial piece. Even without it, the picture that formed frightened her: a future without her beloved son.

"Aye, he rode out this morn. I thought 'twas odd he'd go riding given his illness, but I was so glad to see the back of him, I didna question him."

She clutched Callum's forearm. "Alex threatened to take Alasdair to England without me if I did not obey him. And so he has."

Turning her in his arms, he gripped her shoulders, his gaze boring down upon her. "I will find him. On my life and the love I bear you, I swear I will find them and bear our son safely back. In the meantime, bide you here with Milread and Brie."

Alys shook her head. "He is my son. I want to help. I *can* help."

Brianna draped an arm about her. "My brother-in-law speaks wisdom. Being almost a mother myself, I ken how hard it must be to stay behind and wait, but for now biding here with Milread and me is your best course."

Alys nodded numbly. They were right, of course. Whether she took her own mount or rode with Callum, she would only slow them down.

Feeling useless, she eased out of Callum's arms. "Verra well, I will do as you wish."

HOURS LATER, sitting before the fire in Brianna's solar, Alys could wait no longer. Neither her beloved needlework nor Brianna's reading aloud from *The Canterbury Tales* could take her mind off Alasdair and Callum for so much as a minute.

She set the shirt she was pretending to stitch aside and rose. "I am Alasdair's mother and I am going after them."

She braced herself, expecting them to try and stop her. To her surprise and relief, they didn't.

Brianna rose awkwardly from her brocade-covered chair. "I would that I could ride with you. But in my present state, I am useless."

Milread shoved her runes back in the bag with a sigh. "I would that I was young and fleet of foot."

Brianna added, "I will send some warriors to escort you."

Alys shook her head. Grateful as she was for her friends' care and concern, the time had come for her to stand alone.

"It will take too long to muster them. Besides, Alex will be expecting that. What he will not expect is me."

And why should he? Ere now, she'd been compliant, if not exactly docile. Even after the question about her first marriage arose, still she'd held back and let others do her rescuing. No more.

She left Brianna's chamber for the one she'd shared with Alex. Opening the cupboard, she confirmed his things were indeed gone, including his weapons. Fortunately she still had the dirk Callum had given her. It would suffice.

Folded on the shelf above, she found the set of page's clothes she'd worn seven months before when she and Callum had first met. An inner voice had urged her to hold on to them, mayhap one of Milread's gods whispering in her ear. Now she was glad to have heeded it.

She undressed quickly and put on the snug-fitting hose, trews, doublet coat and high boots. Her coiled hair she stuffed beneath her man's feather-trimmed bonnet cap and slid the dagger in the belted scabbard at her waist.

Brianna and Milread waited for her in the great hall below.

Tears brightened Brie's eyes, which so far as Alys knew was a first. "We've come to see you off." Hugging her, she added, "Godspeed, my friend, and come you back safe. Otherwise this time, my brother-in-law really will do murder—mine." She pulled back and tried for a smile.

More moved than she might say, Alys stepped back from her friend's big belly. "I will, I promise."

Milread tugged on her sleeve. "My Third Eye is opening again. The second sight is not yet back to its full strength and yet still, I see…the wee lad crying upon an English saddle…a copse opening onto a glade with a half-frozen stream running through…a valley below."

Alys and Brianna exchanged looks. From Milread's description, it sounded to be the very spot where seven months before, Brianna's traitorous advisor, Duncan, had tried to murder them. Then Ewan had ridden to the rescue followed closely by Callum. Callum's arrow in Duncan's back had saved Ewan's life. That was the first time Alys had set eyes upon her future love and lord. She'd thought him arrogant, high-handed—and very, very handsome. When he'd lifted her into his arms and set her upon his horse, in her heart she'd known he was The One.

She'd been terrified then, all but frightened of her own shadow and barely able to keep herself in the saddle. She was terrified now, not of falling but of failing. So much stood at stake—her precious child, her precious Callum, and the happy lifetime of never-ending Christmases yet within their reach.

From that time before with Brianna, she was privy to the location of the set of secret stairs at the castle's northwestern quarter. The stone steps led down to a sea gate, a natural escape route. In addition, it also provided a shortcut. Taking it would enable her to recover precious time lost.

It was yet dark when she left the castle. Holding her lantern aloft, she passed the gatehouse and headed for the stables. Her breath struck the air in puffy clouds, her determined footfalls crunching across frost-covered ground.

In the stables, she bypassed her gentle palfrey in its stall and instead opened the gated door to one of Brianna's swiftest steeds. At her direction, the sleepy-eyed groomsmen saddled the horse and walked it over to the mounting block. Alys stepped up to the pedestal, and for the first time she neither hesitated nor shook.

She slid her left foot into the stirrup, missing as the leather loop swung like a noose. It took several attempts, but she finally got her right leg over the horse and swung up into the saddle. She took a moment to get used to the feeling of being so high above ground, and then looped the reins about her gloved hand and locked on to the horse's sides with her thighs and knees.

Retracing the path that she and Brianna had taken during their madcap flight more than seven months ago, she marveled at how much loving Callum had changed her. Seven months ago, she'd barely been able to keep her seat. Seven months ago she likely would have waited for him to return, not because it was the right course but because she would have been too timid to consider striking out on her own. He wasn't the only one of them who was the better for their love. Because of him, she had transformed from a frightened girl to a woman.

At dawn break, her horse stumbled over a rock. Seeking to keep her seat, she felt her foot slip from the stirrup. Seconds later, the earth upended. She fell sideways, landing hard and knocking the breath from her lungs. She scrambled to her feet, forehead and palms bleeding. Fortunately the animal, unharmed, righted itself. Mopping the blood with the back of her glove, she struggled back into the saddle. Her back ached, her thighs ached, and her arms ached, but still she rode on.

Brianna's clan motto was Hold Fast. Until she had Alasdair and Callum back and safe, Alys meant to make it her own, too.

CALLUM ALSO RECALLED the spot where he'd first encountered Alys, which led to the ferry that took passengers across to the mainland. If he were fortunate, his quarry had not yet reached it. The previous night's rain had been a boon for him, for it would have slowed Field's progress. It had also left the back roads moist and in some cases soggy. Once daylight came, he was able to trace the fresh tracks of two horses riding in tandem. Given the scarcity of travelers on the holy days, he had a hunch those tracks belonged to Field and his wife. He prayed to the saints he would be proven right. And that he would find Alasdair yet with them.

He passed through the copse, thinking to stop at the stream and refill his water skein. Raised voices, one of them female, came from the glade ahead. He walked his horse up to the stand of trees. Peeking through the foliage, he saw Field facing off with a gangling, plucked and painted woman, presumably his wife. They stood across from one another at the side of the stream refilling their water skeins. Alasdair rested on a rock between them, chin on his chest, his wee face blotchy from earlier crying but otherwise seemingly unharmed.

Standing on the stream's edge, the woman dipped her skein in the water. "Why should I have to bear the brat on my saddle? He's yours and by the stink of him, his nappy needs changing."

"Because, Morag, you're the woman, that's why. If you're going to pose as his mother, you'd do well to start acting like it."

Holding up her skirts, she snorted. "If you wanted a nursemaid, you should have brought along the bitch that whelped him."

Callum's heart stalled. Thank God Alys was safe back at the castle with Brianna and Milread.

"She was nowhere within the castle and there wasna time to search. And she would be of scant help to us headless."

Standing ankle-deep in the water, Field appeared to have divested himself of his weapons. Callum caught sight of his broad sword propped on a stone precariously close to the boy.

Still, he forced himself to hold back. Not since Ewan had been locked in mortal combat with Duncan had so very much rested on his single shot. He checked to make sure his bracer was in place over his left wrist, his leather shooting glove lined with scarlet covering his right. He took his bow strung with hemp from his shoulder and moved it into position. Shooting a man or woman for that matter was not the same as felling a beast. Reaching down to the quiver of arrows hanging from his waist, he pulled out one of the barbed broad heads, the arrow's cutting edge designed to produce the greatest slashing.

Then and only then did he charge into the clearing.

They swung about to face him, shock replacing the scowls on their faces. For the moment, even Field was rendered speechless. He cast a longing look at the weapon lying beyond arm's reach and cursed.

Callum caught Field's eye and smiled though his heart was drumming. "How now, having the pair of you as quarry makes for verra fine odds indeed."

He was bluffing, of course. He would aim for Alexander. The woman was but a minor player in their passion play. But most importantly, he would not risk hitting the boy.

He shifted his gaze to the woman. "Mistress Field, I presume?" Not waiting for her answer, he said, "Bring me the boy. Otherwise you may be the first to test my hunter's skill."

It seemed there truly was no honor among thieves,

not even wedded ones. She hiked up her skirts and hared off toward the waiting horses. Climbing into the saddle, she dug in her heels and rode off.

Callum returned his attention to Field. "It seems my odds of making my true mark have just improved—greatly."

Field's scarred lip twisted. "I wouldn't count on it, Fraser." He reached down and swept up both Alasdair and his sword. He held the boy in front of him.

Rage ripped through Callum. "You codless scut."

Waking, Alasdair saw him and broke into a wail. "Papa, Papa, come!"

Callum's heart lurched. Taking care to keep his features blank and his voice steady, he called back, "Easy, lad, Papa will fetch you soon." Addressing Alex, he commanded, "Put him down and step away."

"And if I don't."

Callum fitted his arrow into the yew bowstring and took aim. "I am a very good shot."

Alex held Alasdair higher. "You'll have to be."

Field's cowardice disarmed him as another man's bravery never could. "Only the verra vilest of villains would put his own flesh and blood in jeopardy to save his miserable pockmarked hide."

Field didn't deny it. "So, Fraser, what's it going to be? Do you back off and let me ride away or do you bear a bow-riddled corpse back to the fair Alys?"

Callum hesitated. Winning once would have been his most important priority. Rather than release his enemy, he would have taken his chances with Alasdair's life and let his arrow fly. But because of Alys, that arrogant, selfish man was no more. He had become a better man at last. Opening his heart meant opening it to give and receive love as well as to reap hurt. Alasdair was like his own son. A child of his own flesh could not be more precious to him. He hadn't exaggerated when he'd said that he'd give his life for the boy. Even if it meant letting Field go free, keeping his lad safe must be his sole care.

But he would not give up, not yet. Arm tensed and arrow at the ready, he waited, hoping for a distraction for Field—and a Christmas miracle for himself.

ALYS CRESTED THE MOUNTAIN leading to the main traveling road. Woods surrounded her on either side, the close growing trees blocking out sun. Once she'd likened the spot to a witch's forest where the night folk of ghosties and goblins might bide, but she no longer had time or energy to waste on fancies, foolish or otherwise. Her seven-months'-ago self seemed silly to her now. It wasn't the night folk she need fear but the evils of flesh-and-blood men, one man in particular.

Alex Field. Were it not for Alasdair, she would find herself wishing she'd never set eyes upon his face. Fair or foul, he was a monster and she saw now that he always had been. Were his scars to magically disappear, he would remain forever ugly in her eyes.

Here the roads descended into little more than packhorse tracks. The copse was deeper than she recalled. Picking her way through the bracken and closely growing trees made for slow going, but eventually she crested the clearing. Rushing water told her she was not far off from the place.

A horse moving at full gallop sounded ahead. Moments later, horse and rider broke through the trees and came into view. Leaning low in the saddle, the female figure rode toward her as though devils chased her, her cone-shaped cap knocked to one side. Heedless of other passengers, she rode dead center of the narrow road, heading for Alys. Alys made to move to the side and let her pass when the plucked forehead and painted features beneath the headdress came into view. The angular face was chillingly familiar. If Alys lived to be one hundred, never would she forget it. It belonged to the "burgher's widow," the very woman who'd stolen Alasdair seven months before and who likely had helped to steal him this time, too.

And suddenly the final puzzle piece fell into place. The burgher's widow was no widow at all but Alex's lawful, wedded wife.

She took one look at Alys. Plucked forehead furrowing, she wheeled her horse about.

But Alys didn't mean to give up easily. She didn't mean to give up at all. Spurred on by a mother's love, she somehow managed to turn her horse's head and follow suit, quickly building to full gallop. Ere long she and her quarry were riding neck and neck. Struggling to stay in the saddle, she reached across and hauled back a hand. The backhanded blow knocked the bitch from her seat. Reaching across, Alys grabbed the reins. Hands fisted about them, somehow she managed to bring both horses to a halt. Scrambling out of the saddle, she launched herself at the "widow."

They rolled. Alys scrambled atop, pinning the taller,

stronger woman to the ground and pulling her pinkie finger back.

"Ouch!" Sweat broke out on the widow's unnaturally high forehead, and her bony body ceased thrashing. "Get off me."

Harkening back to her borrowed motto, Alys held fast. "Och, I'll get off you all right in good time." She reached down with her free hand and drew out her dirk. Poking the point at the jugular of that knobby white neck, she demanded, "But first, where the hell is my son?"

CALLUM EYED ALEXANDER. Their silent standoff had gone on for longer than he cared to count. Steeling himself to ignore the muscles bunching in his shoulder and the cramping in his forearms, he held his bow and arrow in position, awaiting release. Equally stubborn, Field still held on to the boy. If only there might be some distraction, something to lure the Outlander into lowering his guard and Alasdair if only for a minute.

Horses, two, beat a path toward them. A woman's voice, Morag's, shrilled, "Alex, mind your back!"

Predictably, Field turned. The movement simultaneously shielded Alasdair and made a bull's-eye of Alex's back. Callum didn't hesitate. He drew back and released. Even before the arrow left his bowstring, he knew it would strike sure and true. It did. The steel-tipped head found its target in Alex's left side, his heart's side. Seeing the arrow poking through his front, Field screamed. Callum threw down his bow and swung out of the saddle. He ran over to them, catching Alasdair just as Alex fell sideways into the rock bed.

Clasping Alasdair against his chest, he rubbed soothing circles over the tiny, shuddering shoulders. "There, there, my lad, your papa is here. Dinna fret. You're safe now, my son."

He looked up to see two riders draw up, a young page and Morag. Sporting a black eye and a hatless head, Field's wife sat tethered to the saddle of a second horse, her wrists bound behind her. Taking in the delicate features and shapely legs of the other rider, he realized the page was no page at all. The rider was Alys. She half climbed, half fell from her saddle and rushed over to them.

Twisting his head, Alasdair ceased crying and threw up his chubby arms. "Mama! Mama, come!"

It wasn't until she stood before him that he looked beneath her cap and saw she was hurt. "Alys, love, you're bleeding!"

She dismissed his concern with a flick of her hand. "I took a tumble but I'm fine. Mayhap when you teach Alasdair to ride, you might do the same for me." Despite the cut on her lip, she smiled.

"I think that could be arranged." He handed her the boy and put his arms around them both. "Merry Christmas, my wife."

She sent him a wobbly smile. "Merry Christmas, my husband."

They were still holding on to each other when Ewan, armed to the teeth, rode into the clearing. "What did I miss?" he asked with a grin.

Callum smiled back. "Kidnapping, foiled plotting and one soon-to-be death." He jerked his head to where Field lay twitching.

Ewan dismounted and joined them by Field's prone form. He nudged the fallen man with the toe of his boot. "Care to unburden your soiled soul before you take your leave of this life?"

Alys carried Alasdair a few paces away and set him facing away from the grim view. Retracing her steps to where Field lay, she shook her head. "Why, Alex? I loved you once. Mayhap 'twas only a maid's un-schooled heart I had to offer but had you been kind, had you tended it, that love I felt for you would have grown."

Even with death upon him, Field held fast to his mocking mien. He opened his mouth and laughed. "Love?" He snorted. "What use did I have for the love of a rustic slattern?"

Fury tore through Callum. He stepped forward. Though he'd set his bow aside, he still had the use of his fists. "Were you not already dying, dog, I would make you so for daring to speak of my lady thus. I am minded to finish the business now."

Ewan's hand descended on his shoulder. "No, my brother. He means to goad you into doing that which he desires." He slanted his gaze to Alasdair playing with a pebble along the mound of mud. "Do you really want your son to see you slit a fallen man's throat in cold blood? Let Nature take its course."

Beside him, Alys reached for his fist, unfurled the clenched fingers and slipped her small hand inside. "Ewan has the right of it." Her blue eyes alighted on the fallen man at their feet and her gaze narrowed. "His cruel comments can harm me nay more. And it doesna seem as though he'll live to make those for much longer."

Callum stepped back, reclaiming his calm. They were right, of course. Field could do aught to harm them anymore. His scarred face had lost its florid color and turned ashen and his life's blood was leaking out into the water, turning it pink. Vile words were the rogue's last recourse and like breaths, he hadn't many more left.

Looking up at them, Field laughed. He opened his mouth as if to say more but a wracking cough cut him off. Blood bubbled from the corners of his mouth, dribbling his chin. "You amused me for a time, but once I realized I couldn't rut, 'twas the bairn I cared for."

Between gasping breaths, Alex relayed the rest of his twisted tale. Desperate to get the boy back in order to claim his inheritance, he'd dispatched the "burgher's widow," his wife, Morag, to abduct Alasdair the previous spring. He hadn't counted on insipid little Alys bringing the matter before a laird's court or that anyone in authority would take the word of a whore over that of a seemingly respectable burgher's dame. Once Alys and Alasdair were under the protection of the MacLeod, Alex had to find another way. Fortunately for him, Morag had remained in Skye. Through her, he learned that Alys was affianced to another laird, Callum Fraser.

Standing in a circle around him, Callum, Ewan and Alys exchanged amazed looks. It was quite a tale.

From across the glen, a high-pitched voice called out, "Is he not dead yet? How much longer must we sit about gawking?" Morag, as good as forgotten, scowled at them from where Alys had left her tethered to her horse.

Ewan turned to them and winked. "It seems someone is eager to take up residence in her new home. I think a dungeon cell will do her nicely." He dropped his gaze to Field. "By the looks of him, she will occupy it alone."

Some time later, Ewan rode off with the prisoners, Field strapped facedown over his wife's horse. The danger past and his family finally safe, Callum felt his spirits rising along with a certain member of his anatomy. Stepping back, he glided his gaze over Alys, lingering on her legs. "I recall a twilight eve much as this being the start of our story."

"Aye, my lord. So it was."

Callum angled his face toward her and fastened his hot mouth on the shell of her ear. "Christmas gift giving cuts both ways. Now that we are most proper wed, will you grant me the boon of dressing in breeches betimes? In the privacy of our chamber," he added quickly. He might have become a better man, a man bordering on goodness, but still he wasn't inclined to share.

There was no trace of shyness in the dazzling smile Alys sent him. "Once you have me behind our bolted bed-chamber door, my lord, I will wear as much or as little as you like, be it Christmastide or any other day of the year."

From his seat on the ground, Alasdair called out, "Hung-ar-y!"

Laughing, they walked over to him. Lifting him into his arms, Callum ruffled his golden curls. "Och, that's the settling of it, then. My lady, shall we take our son and return?"

Hand in hand, they walked toward the horses, Callum carrying Alasdair on his shoulders. Now that the danger was past, the boy seemed to view it all as one great silly game. Callum hoped it would always be so. From here on, he meant to devote the rest of his days to making sure that both Alasdair and his mother felt supremely safe and utterly loved.

They were almost to the horses when a beggar burst forth from the bushes. "Ah ha, I have you! Halt you, Callum Fraser, I have you in my sights and by all that is holy you will hear me out."

"You halt, you. Come no further." Wondering how the lunatic came to know his name, Callum handed Alasdair to Alys and set them swiftly behind him. Turning back to the intruder, he unsheathed his dirk.

Wild-eyed, filthy and nearly naked, the man shook his head of matted hair. Ranting of "glad tidings" and "proof positive," he produced a limp wad of parchment from beneath his smock.

"I have glad tidings to report, tidings the Almighty Himself put into my hands to deliver you, and by God you will hear me out even if I must take this stick to your backside to stay you long enough to listen."

Callum slid his knife back in its sheath. "Father Fearghas?"

The priest wagged a grimy finger his way. "Aye, 'tis me or what remains of me. For ten years I bore the burden of your mischief and tricks, Master Fraser, and now that you're a man grown you have managed to finally finish what you began as a wean." He thrust the paper at him. "This page I took from the parish records with mine own hands. The Lady Alys is not married to any man save to you. Alexander Field was already wed when first they met. The parish records prove his wedding well enough but to another lady. The marriage to milady was a sham, a vicious ruse. This is the proof of it. Take it, take it, *please!*"

Stepping around to Callum's side, Alys said very gently, "Aye, Father, we know."

The priest's eyes popped. "You…know?"

She nodded. "Alexander confessed all."

Father Fearghas crushed the paper in his fist. "You know!" He slammed the wad upon the ground and stamped it beneath his bare and bruised heel. Jumping up and down, he shrieked, "You know! You know! Do you ken what I have endured this past week? Do you?"

Callum and Alys shook their heads. Cautiously Callum said, "It seems you have suffered some…ill?"

"Some…ill?" Father Fearghas pulled at the neck of his smock. "Since last I left you, Callum Fraser, I have been poisoned by bad food, beset with the gripes, beaten, robbed and ridiculed. I have humbled myself before my sister and endured her taunts and gloating. I have deceived a fellow priest and defaced a parish records book. I, who set out to walk in the footsteps of Christian saints and martyrs, will find myself fortunate if I am not defrocked. All these trials and tribulations I have endured for naught—because you know!"

His head fell. His shoulders sagged. He looked to be on the verge of crying.

Callum and Alys exchanged looks. Beneath her breath, she cautioned, "Be gentle with him."

Callum nodded. He stepped up to his old tutor and extended his hand. "Thank you."

Coming up on the priest's other side, Alys reached out with her free hand and patted his shoulder. "Yes, good father, thank you. If 'tis any consolation, we only learned the full truth mere moments ago."

Father Fearghas jerked up his head, the wild look once more upon him. "You mean to say I missed the opportunity to be the bearer of glad tidings, the messenger of the Almighty, and the hero of this godforsaken tale by mere…moments?"

Callum and Alys hesitated. Alys spoke up, "Good news is always welcome news." She punctuated the pronouncement with a bright smile.

Later Father Fearghas would recall that in that moment he'd felt a great rumbling inside him, not his belly this time but higher up, in his chest. Along with it came a tickling sensation moving into his throat as if an unseen feather were sweeping across his palate.

To everyone's astonishment, including his, he dropped to his knees, threw back his head—and laughed.

Epilogue

THEY MARRIED AGAIN on Twelfth Night, not out of need but so that all their loved ones might be present to share in their joy. Ewan and Brianna hosted the celebration. Their chapel and great hall were festooned with flowers and bows of yew and holly for the occasion and a much restored Father Fearghas once again officiated over the saying of the vows. After the ceremony, they filed back into the great hall for the feasting. Milread performed another rune cast as a gift for the newlyweds. Given how matters had gone the last time, Alys hesitated but Callum accepted with alacrity if only, Alys suspected, to tweak Father Fearghas.

This time the rune cast brought forth a glowingly positive report, the presence and position of the ancient symbols foretelling of fertility and bright new beginnings. According to Milread, the prominent presence of BEORC, the rune of birth and family, almost always foretold of a babe soon to come. Alys slipped a hand below the table, laid it upon her flat belly and smiled to herself. It was too soon to be certain, just a feeling she had, but she strongly suspected that part of the prophecy was already on its way to coming true.

Fittingly the final rune was WUNJO, the rune representing joy and Happily Ever After.

Now many hours later, the feasting was at last showing signs of winding down. Torches lit one end of the chamber to the other. From the minstrel's gallery, fiddlers and pipers and drummers played on and likely would do so well into the night and next morn. The guests having sated themselves with every imaginable dish of food and form of drink, the trestle tables were moved to the side to make way for the entertainment.

With an exchange of looks, Callum and Ewan excused themselves from the head table and descended the dais to the floor.

Ewan called the company to silence. "My brother, the Fraser, and I will perform the Highland Fling for the honor and entertainment of our respective fair ladies."

Alys leaned over to Brianna and whispered, "Did you know of this?"

Brianna shook her head. "Ewan said something about a shared Christmas gift but that is all I could wrest from him."

Servants materialized from the room's far corners. Two round spiked battle shields were laid in the center of the floor, one before each man. Stripped down to their shirts and kilts, the brothers Fraser turned to each other and bowed.

Callum grinned. "Let the games begin, brother."

The bagpipes began. Each man leapt atop his shield. Fisted hands resting on their hips, stances lance straight, and feet flying, they danced. Taking in the complicated heel-to-toe kicks, Alys marveled at how they managed to avoid the sharp spike of steel in each shield's center. Never before had she seen the like. It was quickly clear that the performance was not so much dance as sport and that sibling rivalry had not ended with age. Sweat poured from brows as each brother sought to outdo the other in daring and dexterity and grace. Alys supposed that to an impartial observer the twins would appear evenly matched in looks and form, but to her eyes Callum was the clear victor, the shining star.

Shouts of "huzzah" rose about the room amidst wild clapping. Beaming, each brother stepped off his shield and bowed to his lady.

Returning to her side, Callum went down on bended knee before her. Ewan rendered the same honor to Brianna, but Alys's eyes were firmly fixed on her lord. "I ken you are full of gifts and surprises, my lord."

Heedless of who might be watching, Callum took her hands between his and kissed the tips of her fingers. Looking up at her through his dark lashes, the smile he sent her rivaled the brilliance of any sunbeam she'd so far seen. "If I'm to make every day from here on Christmas, then so I must be."

Not long later, he carried her up the spiraling stairs to their chamber and laid her in the center of the big wood-framed bed. Looking up at him, she sighed. "After all that has passed, my lord, I still canna credit that I'm not dreaming, that I can trust all this happiness to be true."

Field had survived the journey back to Castle MacLeod but barely. Within an hour of his arrival, he was dead. Eager to better her lot by diverting blame, Morag confirmed all that he'd told them in the glen. The burgher's widow, who was now a widow in truth, still bided in Brianna's dungeon. Come spring, however, she could look forward to a surfeit of fresh air and sunshine—making bricks in Brianna's mud pit.

Callum came down on the bed beside her and gathered her into his arms. "It's true, my dearling. Heretofore you can trust in the future—and me."

He leaned over and kissed her. Sweet, soft and abidingly tender, it was but the prelude to a lifetime of not only kisses but lovemaking and loving to come.

Drawing back, he touched her tear-wet cheek with gentle fingers. "I promised you not only a Twelvetide of pleasure but beyond it, a lifetime of Christmases, did I not? And I mean to make up for our lost holy days starting…now. Only Alys, my dearling, now that we are well wedded and soon to be even better bedded, do you nay ken you might commence calling me by my given name? Do you ken you might call me Callum?" He punctuated the request with a wink.

"Aye, I will and I can." Smiling, she stroked her hand down his lean cheek. "To whit, I bid you a verra merry Christmas, my husband, my love, my Callum, and a most magick-filled new year."

* * *

'THIS EVENING I'm flying to New York for two weeks,'
Jasim imparted with a casualness that made her heart sink
like a stone. 'That's why I had you brought here. I own this
apartment and you'll be comfortable here while I'm abroad.'

'I can afford my own accommodation although I may not
need it for long. I'll have another job by the time you
get back—'

Jasim released a slightly harsh laugh. 'There's no need for
you to look for another position. How would I ever see you?
Don't you understand what I'm offering you?'

Elinor stood very still. 'No, I must be incredibly thick
because I haven't quite worked out yet what you're offering
me....'

His charismatic smile slashed his lean dark visage.
'Naturally, I want to take care of you....'

'No, thanks.' Elinor forced a smile and mentally willed him not to demean her with some sordid proposition. 'The only man who will ever take *care* of me with my agreement will be my husband. I'm willing to wait for you to come back but I'm not willing to be kept by you. I'm a very independent woman and what I give, I give freely.'

Jasim frowned. 'You make it all sound so serious.'

'What happened between us last night left pure chaos in its wake. Right now, I don't know whether I'm on my head or my heels. I'll stay for a while because I have nowhere else to go in the short term. So maybe it's good that you'll be away for a while.'

Jasim pulled out his wallet to extract a card. 'My private number,' he told her, presenting her with it as though it was a precious gift, which indeed it was. Many women would have done just about anything to gain access to that direct hotline to him, but his staff guarded his privacy with scrupulous care.

Before he could close the wallet, his blood ran cold in his veins. How could he have made such a serious oversight? What if he had got her pregnant? He knew that an unplanned pregnancy would engulf his life like an avalanche, crush his freedom and suffocate him. He barely stilled a shudder at the threat of such an outcome and thought how ironic it was that what his older brother had longed and prayed for to secure the line to the throne should strike Jasim as an absolute disaster....

* * *

What will proud Prince Jasim do if Elinor is expecting his royal baby? Perhaps an arranged marriage is the only solution! But will Elinor agree? Find out in DESERT PRINCE, BRIDE OF INNOCENCE by Lynne Graham [#2884], available from Harlequin Presents® in January 2010.

REQUEST YOUR FREE BOOKS!

2 FREE NOVELS PLUS 2 FREE GIFTS!

HARLEQUIN®

Blaze

Red-hot reads!

HB09R3

COMING NEXT MONTH

Available December 29, 2009

#513 BLAZING BEDTIME STORIES, VOLUME III Tori Carrington and Tawny Weber
Bedtime Stories
What better way to spend an evening than cuddling up with your better half, indulging in supersexy fairy tales? We guarantee that sleeping will be the last thing on your mind!

#514 MOONSTRUCK Julie Kenner
Claire Daniels is determined to get her old boyfriend back. She's tired of being manless, especially during the holidays, and she'd like nothing more than a New Year's Eve kiss to start the year off right. And she gets just that. Too bad it's not her ex-boyfriend she's kissing…

#515 MIDNIGHT RESOLUTIONS Kathleen O'Reilly
Where You Least Expect It
A sudden, special kiss between two strangers in Times Square on New Year's Eve turns unforgettable, and soon Rose Hildebrande and Ian Cumberland's sexy affair is smokin' hot despite the frosty weather. Will things cool off, though, once the holiday season ends?

#516 SEXY MS. TAKES Jo Leigh
Encounters
It's New Year's Eve in Manhattan and the ball is about to drop in Times Square…. Bella, Willow and Maggie are on their way to the same blockbuster Broadway audition until fate—and three very sexy men—sideline their journey with sizzling results!

#517 HER SECRET FLING Sarah Mayberry
Don't dip your pen in the office ink. Good advice for rookie columnist Poppy Birmingham. Too bad coworker Jake Stevens isn't listening. Their recent road trip has turned things from antagonistic to hedonistic! He wants to keep this fling on the down-low…but with heat this intense, that's almost impossible.

#518 HIS FINAL SEDUCTION Lori Wilde
Signing up for an erotic fantasy vacation was Jorgina Gerard's ticket to reinventing herself. The staid accountant was more than ready for a change, but has she taken on too much when she meets and seduces the hot, very gorgeous every-woman-would-want-him Quint Mason? She's looking forward to finding out!